"Stand up."

Callie blinked. "What?"

His dark eyes glittered as raindrops splattered noisily into the trees above. "You heard me."

She sucked in her breath as fury and fear raced through her. "Forget it! You have no power over me. I'm no longer your secretary, and I'm certainly not your lover. I'm your nothing! I don't know why you came looking for me, but I want you to go away and leave me alone!"

Eduardo came very, very close, standing over her on the stoop, so close his pant legs brushed her knees. He leaned in to her, and she felt the warmth of his breath against her earlobe as he whispered, "Are you pregnant with my baby, Callie?"

Jennie Lucas grew up dreaming about faraway lands. At fifteen, hungry for experience beyond the borders of her small Idaho city, she went to a Connecticut boarding school on scholarship. She took her first solo trip to Europe at sixteen, then put off college and travelled around the US, supporting herself with jobs as diverse as gas station cashier and newspaper advertising assistant.

At twenty-two she met the man who would be her husband. After their marriage she graduated from Kent State with a degree in English. Seven years after she started writing she got the magical call from London that turned her into a published author.

Since then life has been hectic, with a new writing career, a sexy husband and two small children, but she's having a wonderful (albeit sleepless) time. She loves immersing herself in dramatic, glamorous, passionate stories. Maybe she can't physically travel to Morocco or Spain right now, but for a few hours a day, while her children are sleeping, she can be there in her books.

Jennie loves to hear from her readers. You can visit her website at www.jennielucas.com, or drop her a note at jennie@jennielucas.com

Recent titles by the same author:

A NIGHT OF LIVING DANGEROUSLY
RECKLESS NIGHT IN RIO
THE VIRGIN'S CHOICE

**Did you know these are also available as eBooks?
Visit www.millsandboon.co.uk**

TO LOVE, HONOUR AND BETRAY

BY
JENNIE LUCAS

First published in Great Britain 2012
by Mills & Boon, an imprint of Harlequin (UK) Limited.
Harlequin (UK) Limited, Eton House, 18-24 Paradise Road,
Richmond, Surrey TW9 1SR

© Jennie Lucas 2012

ISBN: 978 0 263 22748 2

Harlequin (UK) policy is to use papers that are natural, renewable and recyclable products and made from wood grown in sustainable forests. The logging and manufacturing process conform to the legal environmental regulations of the country of origin.

Printed and bound in Great Britain
by CPI Antony Rowe, Chippenham, Wiltshire

TO LOVE, HONOUR AND BETRAY

To my husband.

Thanks for Europe.

Thanks even more for home.

Thanks for making all my dreams come true.

CHAPTER ONE

CALLIE WOODVILLE had dreamed of her wedding day since she was a little girl.

When she was seven, she placed a long white towel on her head and walked down an imaginary aisle in her father's barn, surrounded by teddy bears as guests and with her baby sister toddling behind her, chewing on flower petals from a basket.

At seventeen, as a plump, bookish wallflower with big glasses and clothes hand-sewn by her loving but sadly out-of-date mother, Callie was mocked and ignored by the boys at her rural high school. She told herself she didn't care. She went to prom with her best friend instead, an equally nerdy boy from a neighboring farm. But Callie dreamed of the day she would finally meet the darkly handsome man she could love. She knew that somewhere out there in the wide world, he waited for her, this man who would wake her with the sensual power of his kiss.

Then, when she was twenty-four, that man had come for her.

Her ruthless billionaire boss had kissed her. Seduced her. He'd taken her virginity, as he'd already taken her heart, and for one perfect night she was lost in passion and magic. Waking up in his arms on Christmas morning, in the luxurious bedroom of his New York brownstone,

Callie thought she might die of pure happiness. For that one perfect night, the world was a magical place where dreams came true, as long as your heart was pure and you truly believed.

One magical, heartbreaking night.

Now, eight and a half months later, Callie sat on the stoop outside her former apartment on a leafy, quiet street in the West Village. The sky was dark, threatening rain, and though it was early September it was hot and muggy. But her cleaned-out apartment felt almost ghostly in its emptiness, so she'd come outside to wait with the suitcases.

Today was her wedding day. The day she'd always dreamed of. But she'd never dreamed of this.

Callie looked down at her secondhand wedding dress and the wilting bouquet of wildflowers she'd picked from the nearby community garden. Instead of a veil, pearl-laced barrettes strained to hold back her long, light brown hair.

In a few minutes, she'd marry her best friend. A man she'd never kissed—or even *wanted* to kiss. A man who wasn't the father of her baby.

As soon as Brandon came back with the rental car, they'd be wed at City Hall, and start the long drive from New York to his parents' farm in North Dakota.

Callie closed her eyes. *It's best for the baby,* she told herself desperately. Her baby needed a father, and her ex-boss was a selfish, coldhearted playboy, whose deepest relationship was with his bank account. After three years of devoted service as his secretary, Callie had known that. But she'd still been stupid enough to find out the hard way.

A car turned off Seventh Avenue onto her residential street in the West Village. She saw an expensive dark luxury sedan and watched it go by, then exhaled. It wasn't Eduardo's style of car, and yet, as clouds covered the noonday sun, Callie looked up at the sky and shivered. If her ex-boss ever found out their single night of passion had created a child…

"He won't," she whispered aloud. Last she'd heard, he was in Colombia, developing offshore oil fields for Cruz Oil. After Eduardo possessed a woman in bed, she was pretty much dead to him, never to be remembered again. And though Callie had witnessed this scores of times during her time as his secretary, she'd still thought that she might be different. That she would be the exception.

Get out of my bed, Callie. She'd still been naked and blissful and sleepy in the pink light of Christmas morning when he'd shaken her awake, his voice hard. *Get out of my house. I'm through with you.*

Eight and a half months later, his words were still an ice pick in her heart. Exhaling, Callie wrapped her arms around her baby bump. He would never know about the life he'd created inside her. He'd made his choice. So she'd made hers. There would be no custody battle, no chance for Eduardo to be as domineering and tyrannical a father as he'd been a boss. Her child would be born into a stable home, with a loving family. Brandon, her best friend since the first grade, would be her baby's father in all the ways that counted, and Callie would be a devoted wife to him in return. In every way but one.

She'd been doubtful at first that a marriage based on friendship could work. But Brandon had assured her that they didn't need romance or passion to have a solid partnership. "We'll be happy, Callie," he'd promised. "Really happy." Over the months of her pregnancy, he'd worn her down with kindness.

Now, as Callie leaned back against their suitcases on the stoop, her eyes fell on her Louis Vuitton handbag. Brandon kept telling her to sell it. It would look ridiculous on the farm, she knew. It had been a gift from Eduardo last Christmas. *Totally unnecessary*, she'd wept, amazed that he'd noticed her gaze lingering upon the shop window months before. *I reward those who are loyal to me, Callie,* Eduardo had replied. *A woman like you comes along only once in a lifetime.*

Squeezing her eyes shut, Callie turned her face upward, feeling the first cool raindrops against her skin. Such a ridiculous trophy, a three-thousand-dollar handbag, but it had been a hard-won symbol of her hours of devotion, of their partnership. But Brandon was right. She should just sell it. She was done with Eduardo. With New York. Done with everything she'd once loved.

Except this baby.

A low roll of thunder mingled with the honk of taxis and distant police sirens on Seventh Avenue and the hiss from the subway vent at the end of the street. She heard another car pull down the street. It stopped, and she heard a door slam. Brandon had returned with the rental car. It was time to marry him and start the two-day journey to North Dakota. Forcing her lips into a smile, she opened her eyes.

Eduardo Cruz stood beside his dark Mercedes sedan, powerful and broad-shouldered in an impeccable black suit.

The blood drained from Callie's cheeks.

"Eduardo," she breathed, starting to rise. She stopped herself. Maybe he couldn't see her pregnant belly. She prayed he couldn't. Wrapping her arms loosely over her knees, she stammered, "What are you doing here?"

Silently Eduardo stepped onto the sidewalk. His long-limbed, powerful body moved toward her with a warrior's effortless grace, but she felt every step like a seismic rumble beneath her.

"The question is—" his dark eyes glittered "—what are *you* doing, Callie?"

His voice was deep, with only a hint of an accent from his childhood in Spain. It was a shock to hear that voice again. She'd never thought she would see him again, outside of her haunted, sensual dreams.

She lifted her chin. "What does it look like I'm doing?" She jabbed her thumb toward the suitcases. "Leaving." Her voice trembled in spite of her best efforts, and she hated Eduardo for that, as she hated him for so much else. "You've won."

"Won?" he ground out. He slowly circled her at the end of the stoop. "A strange accusation."

Beneath his gaze, her body shuddered with ice, then fire. She stiffened, glaring at him. "What else would you call it? You fired me then made sure no one else in New York would hire me."

"So?" he said coldly. "Let McLinn provide for you. You are his bride. His problem."

A chill went down her spine.

"You know about Brandon?" she whispered. If he knew about her coming marriage, did he also know about her pregnancy? "Who told you?"

"He did." He gave a harsh laugh. "I met him."

"You met? When? Where?"

Eduardo gave her a hard smile. "Does it matter?"

She bit her lip. "Was it a chance meeting…or…"

"You might call it chance." His casual drawl belied the cold accusation in his eyes. He looked up at the expensive town house behind her. "I stopped by your apartment and was surprised to find you had a live-in lover."

"He's not my—"

"Not your what?"

"Never mind," she mumbled.

Eduardo moved closer. "Tell me," he said acidly, "did McLinn enjoy living here? Did he relish living in the apartment I leased as a gift of gratitude for the secretary I respected?"

She swallowed. A year ago, she'd been living in a cheap studio in Staten Island, so she could send most of her salary to her family back home. Then Eduardo had surprised her with a paid yearlong lease for a gorgeous one-bedroom apartment close to his own expensive brownstone on Bank Street. Callie had nearly wept with joy, believing it was proof that he actually cared. She'd later realized he'd only wanted to eliminate her commute so he could get more hours out of her.

"What could you possibly have to say to me now?" She frowned. She'd been home all week—packing boxes, directing the movers, being informed by the airlines that she was too pregnant to fly, calling car rental agencies. "When were you even here?"

"While you were in bed," Eduardo ground out.

Her heart lifted to her throat.

"Oh," she whispered. It suddenly made sense. She slept in the bedroom, while Brandon had the couch. "He never mentioned meeting you. But why? What do you want?"

His black eyes glittered at her. He was staring at her as if she were a stranger. No—as if she were a bug beneath his Italian leather shoe. "Why didn't you ever tell me about your lover? Why did you lie?"

"I didn't!"

"You hid his existence from me. The very day after you moved into this apartment, you had him move in with you. But you never mentioned him, because you knew it would make me question your commitment and loyalty."

She stared at him then her shoulders sagged. "I was

afraid to tell you." She swallowed. "You're so unreasonable in your demand for absolute loyalty."

His mouth was a grim line. "So you lied."

"I never invited him to move in! He…he surprised me." After Callie had called Brandon in North Dakota to tell him about the apartment her generous boss had just leased for her, he'd shown up on her doorstep the next day, telling her he was worried about her in the big city. "He missed me. He was going to get his own place, but then he couldn't find a job.…"

"Right," Eduardo said sardonically. "A real man finds a job to support his woman. He doesn't live off her severance package."

She gasped at the insult. "He's not like that!" Throughout her pregnancy, Brandon had cooked, cleaned, rubbed her swollen feet, held her hand at the doctor's office. All the things that she'd have wanted her baby's real father to do, if he'd been anyone besides Eduardo. She scowled. "In case you haven't noticed, there aren't many jobs in New York for *farmers!*"

"So why stay in New York?"

Soft, lazy raindrops fell around them, pattering against the hot sidewalk. "I wanted to stay. I hoped I would find a job."

"And so you have. As a farmer's wife."

"What do you want from me? Why did you come— just to insult me?"

"Oh, didn't I mention why?" His eyes were cold and black. "Your sister called me this morning."

A chill went through her.

"Sami—called you?" Callie's conversation with her sister last night had ended badly. But Sami wouldn't betray her. She wouldn't…would she? She licked her suddenly dry lips. "Um. What did she say?"

"Two very interesting things that I could hardly believe." Eduardo took a step closer to her on the stoop and said softly, "But clearly one of them is true. You're getting married today."

Her body started to shake. "So?"

"You admit it?"

"I'm wearing a wedding gown. I can't exactly deny it. But how does that affect you?" Her lips trembled as she tried to shape them into a mocking smile. "Mad because you weren't invited?"

"You sound nervous." He slowly walked a semicircle around the end of the stoop. "Is there something you are keeping from me, Callie? Some secret?" He moved closer. "Some lie?"

She felt a contraction across her body, her belly tightening. Braxton-Hicks contractions, caused by stress, she told herself. Fake labor, the same that had sent her racing to the hospital last week, only to have the nurses sigh and send her home. But it hurt. One hand went over her belly; the other went to her lower back as she panted, "What could I possibly have to hide?"

"I already know you're a liar." A beam of golden light escaped the gray clouds and caressed his handsome face, leaving dark shadows beneath his cheekbones and jawline as he said softly, "But how deep do your lies go?"

The wilted bouquet of wildflowers nearly fell from her numb fingers. She gripped them more tightly in her shaking hands. "Please," she whispered. "Don't ruin it."

"Ruin—what—exactly?"

Her teeth chattered. "My...my..." *My life. And my baby's life.* "My wedding day."

"Ah, yes. Your wedding day. I know how you used to dream about it." He looked down at her. "So tell me. Is it everything you hoped it would be?"

She felt painfully conscious of the used wedding dress, several sizes too large, with a lace and polyester bodice that kept sliding off one shoulder. She looked down at the wilting flowers, at the two shabby suitcases behind her.

"Yes," she said in a small voice.

"Where is your family? Where are your friends?"

"We're getting married at City Hall." She lifted her chin defiantly, pushing aside the sudden desire to cry. "We're eloping. It's romantic."

"Ah. Of course." He showed his teeth in a smile. "The wedding would not matter to you and McLinn, would it, as long as you have your honeymoon."

Honeymoon? She and Brandon planned to break up their drive on a pull-out sofa at his cousin's house in Wisconsin. Passion was nonexistent between them—she thought of Brandon like a brother. But she could hardly admit to Eduardo that there was only one man on earth she'd ever wanted to kiss, only one man she'd ever dreamed about: the man glaring cold daggers at her right now. "My honeymoon is none of your business."

Eduardo snorted. "Anything for you would be romantic where Brandon McLinn is concerned. Even an ugly dress and a bouquet of weeds. He's always been the one you wanted. Even though he is a man without a job, unable to stand on his own two feet. You *love* him—" his voice was scornful "—though he is barely a man."

Callie's jaw clenched. She started to rise to her feet then she remembered she couldn't let him see her belly. Trembling with fury, she glared up at him. "Rich or poor, Brandon is twice the man you'll ever be!"

Eduardo's eyes burned through her. Then he spoke coldly.

"Stand up."

She blinked. "What?"

"Your sister told me two things. The first is true." Raindrops splattered noisily into the trees above. "Stand up."

Callie sucked in her breath. "Forget it! I'm not your secretary, I'm not your lover…I'm your *nothing*! You have no power over me, not anymore. Stop harassing me before I call the police!"

Eduardo's dark eyes glittered as he moved closer, standing over her, so close his pant legs brushed her knees. He leaned forward. "Are you pregnant with my baby?"

Staring up at him, Callie sucked in her breath. He *knew*.

Her sister had betrayed her. She'd told Eduardo everything.

She'd known Sami was angry, but she'd never thought she'd do it. Yesterday, her sister had called to wish her good luck on her trip. Callie had been jittery and afraid she was about to make the worst mistake of her life. When she'd heard her sister's loving voice, she'd blurted out her plan to elope with Brandon because she was pregnant by her boss. Sami's reaction had been furious.

I won't let you trap Brandon this way, with a baby that's not even his!

Sami, you don't understand –

Shut up! Even if your old boss is a jerk, it's his baby and he deserves to know! I won't let you ruin so many lives with your selfishness!

Callie had been shocked, but she'd never once thought Sami would go through with her threat. Her baby sister adored her. She'd trailed after Callie and Brandon every day for years with hero worship in her eyes. She might be angry, but she'd certainly never betray her. Or so she'd thought.

She'd been wrong.

"Are you?" Eduardo demanded harshly.

Callie felt another hard contraction. She tried to breathe through it, but the childbirth classes she'd attended with Brandon seemed useless. The fake contractions, which were supposed to get her body ready for eventual labor weeks in the future, were getting stronger.

"Very well. Do not answer," Eduardo said coldly. "I would not believe a word from your lying mouth, in any case. But your body..." He stroked her cheek, and an electric current coursed through her. Callie looked up with a gasp, her lips parted. "Your body won't lie to me."

He removed the bouquet of wildflowers from her unresisting hand and dropped it to the ground. Taking both her hands in his own, palm to palm, he gently lifted her to her feet.

Callie stood before him on the sidewalk, shaking and vulnerable and clearly pregnant in an ugly white wedding dress. Closing her eyes, she waited for the explosion.

But when he spoke, his voice was cool. "So it is true. You are pregnant." He paused. "Who is the father?"

Her eyes flew open. "What?" she stammered.

"Is it me? Or McLinn?"

"How can you ask...?" She faltered, blushing. "You know I was a virgin when we...when we..."

"I thought you were, though I wondered later if I'd been deceived." He set his jaw. "Perhaps you were saving yourself for your wedding night, and the day after we made love, you went home to your fiancé, and lured him into bed. Perhaps in a fit of remorse, or perhaps to hide what you'd done in case there was a child."

"How can you even say that?" she gasped. "How can you think I'd do something so disgusting—so low?"

"Is the child is mine? Or is it McLinn's?" His gaze was like ice. His sensual lips twisted. "Or do you not know?"

Her heart wrenched.

"Why are you trying to hurt me?" She shook her head. "Brandon is my friend. Just my friend."

"You've been living with him for a year. Do you expect me to believe he slept on the couch for all that time?"

"We took turns!"

"You are lying! He is *marrying* you!"

"Out of kindness, nothing more!"

He gave a harsh laugh. "*Por supuesto*," he mocked, folding his arms. "That is why men marry. To be *kind.*"

She stepped back from him. Her throat throbbed with anguish. "My parents don't know I'm pregnant. They think I've just given up the job hunt and decided to move home." Her eyes burned as she shook her head fiercely. "I can't go back there as an unwed mother. My parents would never live it down. And Brandon is the best man on earth. He—"

"I don't give a damn about him. Or you. I care about one question. Is. This. Baby. Mine?"

Callie took a deep breath. "Please don't," she whispered. She despised the pleading note in her voice but couldn't stop herself. "Don't make me give you an answer you don't want. Let me give her a home. A family."

"Her?"

She could have kicked herself. Reluctantly she looked at him. "I'm having a baby girl."

He exhaled, setting his jaw. "A girl."

"It doesn't matter! You don't want to be tied to me. You've made that clear! She's nothing to you, any more than I am. You must forget you ever saw me—"

"Are you out of your mind?" he growled, grabbing her shoulders. "I won't let another man raise a child that could be mine!" He searched her gaze fiercely. "When is the baby due? What is the exact date?"

Thunder rolled across the dark clouds hanging low over

the city. Callie felt herself on a precipice of a choice that would change everything.

If she told Eduardo the truth, her baby would never enjoy the idyllic childhood that Callie had had, surrounded by endless prairie, playing in her father's barn, knowing everyone in their small town. Instead of parents who were best friends, her precious child would have parents who hated each other, and a tyrannical, selfish father.

If only she were the liar Eduardo thought she was, Callie thought miserably. If only she could give him a false date, and say Brandon was the father!

But she couldn't lie. Not to his face. Especially not about something like this. Grief twisted her heart as she whispered, "September 17."

Eduardo stared down at her. Then his eyes narrowed and the grip on her shoulders tightened.

"If there's even the slightest chance McLinn is the father, tell me now," he ground out. "Before the paternity test. If you're lying—or if you are simply wrong—and this baby is not mine, I will destroy you for your lie. Do you understand? Not just you, but everyone who loves you. Especially McLinn."

Her throat ached. She knew her ex-boss's ruthlessness. She'd seen him use it against others for three years, and finally—inevitably—against her. "I would expect nothing less."

"I will take your parents' farm. McLinn's. Everything. Do you understand?" His dark eyes glittered. "So choose your words carefully. Tell me the truth. Am I the—"

"Of course!" she exploded. "Of course you're the father! You're the only man I've ever slept with! Ever!"

Staggering back a step, Eduardo stared down at her. His jaw hardened. "*Still*? Do you honestly expect me to believe that?"

"Why would I lie? Do you think I actually *want* you to be her father?" she cried. "I wish with all my heart it was Brandon, not you! He's the one I want—the one I trust—the best man in the world! Instead of a selfish workaholic playboy who turns on everyone in his life, who doesn't trust anyone, who has no real friends—"

Her voice cut off as his fingers tightened into her flesh. "You were never going to tell me about the baby, were you?" His voice was dangerously soft. "You were just going to steal my child from me and put another man in my place. You were going to erase me completely from her life."

A shiver of fear went through her, but she glared at him. "Yes! She'd be better off without you!"

He sucked in his breath then bared his teeth into a smile.

"And that," he said, his black eyes gleaming, "is your greatest lie of all."

They stood glaring at each other on the sidewalk, like mortal enemies. She heard the soft patter of heavy rain-drops sliding from the green leafy trees above the brick town houses, and she knew he was right.

For eight months, Callie had told herself that Eduardo wouldn't want a baby. That his workaholic bachelor life-style would be hampered by a child. That he would be a horrible father and she was doing the right thing for everyone. But part of her had always known that wasn't true. After being orphaned himself, and brought to New York at the age of ten, Eduardo Cruz would want to be a father. He'd never surrender a son or daughter.

It was just *Callie* he would sweep aside and discard.

And that was what frightened her. With Eduardo Cruz's wealth and power, if he took her to court to battle for full custody, there was no question who would win.

His dark eyes cut her to the bone. "You should have told me the day you realized you were pregnant."

She looked up at him, her heart twisting beneath the weight of guilt and regret and the grief of broken love. "How could I," she whispered, "after you abandoned me?"

His eyes widened. Then he glowered at her, his expression merciless. "You are clever and resourceful. You could have found a way to contact me. But you did not. You tried to hide her, as you hide everything."

She felt another sharp pain as her belly tightened. "And now I've told you the truth, will you try to take her from me?"

His jaw tightened. Then a smile curled his lips. Reaching out his hand, he stroked her cheek. A sizzle of electricity spun across her skin, vibrating down her spine, and she was filled with longing and desire, irrepressible need like fire. All her traitorous body wanted to do, even now, was turn toward him like a flower toward the sun.

"You will be punished, *querida*," he said softly. "Oh, yes."

Callie stared up at him, breathless beneath his touch, trapped beneath the dark force of his gaze. Then she exhaled when she saw a cheap two-door hatchback driving up her street. The cavalry had come to save her. She nearly sobbed with relief. "Brandon!"

Eduardo whipped around. A low, guttural word came from his lips, a word in Spanish she'd only heard him use when he'd just lost a huge deal, or the time a brokenhearted starlet had tried to break into his bedroom. Turning back, he grabbed Callie's handbag, then her arm. "Come with me."

Before she even knew what was happening, he'd pulled her across the sidewalk and opened the back door to his black sedan. "Start the engine," he ordered his driver.

Realizing his intent, she desperately tried to rip her arm away. "Let me go!"

But Eduardo's grip was like steel. He shoved her into the backseat and climbed in beside her, crowding her with his massive body that seemed far too big for the space.

Eduardo leaned over her, his eyes black with fury as he gripped her wrists. "I'm not giving you another chance to hide my baby."

Callie breathed in the woodsy, exotic scent of his cologne, overwhelmed by his closeness, by the sensation of his thigh pressed against hers. It was just as she'd dreamed about in the years she'd worked for him, and unwillingly dreamed every night in all the months since he'd fired her. Their faces were inches apart. Callie's heart thumped in her chest. She felt lost in a dream.

Then Eduardo closed the door with a bang behind him.

"Drive," he told his chauffeur tersely.

"No!" With an intake of breath, she whirled around in the backseat. Her last vision through the back window was of Brandon standing by the rental car with his door ajar, staring after her with his black-framed glasses askew, his expression anguished. Beside him, their two old suitcases still sat forlornly on the curb.

Their car turned the corner, and Brandon was gone. Callie's body felt tight with pain that seemed to emanate white-hot from her heart as she turned back to Eduardo with a choked sob. "Take me back. Please."

His eyes were merciless. "No."

"You've kidnapped me!"

"Call it what you want."

"You can't keep me against my will!"

"Can't I?" he said softly.

She shivered at the look in his eyes. He turned away

as if bored, but she saw the hard set of his jaw, heard the clipped tension of his voice as he said coldly, "You will remain with me until the matter of the baby is resolved."

"So I'm your prisoner?"

"Until my paternal rights are formalized—yes."

"So you don't believe I'm a liar after all," Callie said bitterly.

"Not about the baby. But there are all kinds of lying. You lie with silence. I wonder," he said blandly, "if there's anything else you've been hiding from me? My perfect, loyal secretary."

She wrapped her arms over her belly, which felt hard and tight beneath the polyester blend of her wedding dress. "What do you know about loyalty? You've never been loyal to anyone but yourself!"

"I was loyal to you, Callie," he said in a low voice. "Once."

Staring into his fathomless dark eyes, she was suddenly lost in memories of their days together, in the office, sharing sushi at midnight, traveling the world on his private jet.

"That was when I mistakenly believed you were worth it." His tone hardened. "I learned my lesson."

"What lesson?" she cried out, bewildered. "The instant I slept with you, I went from being your trusted secretary to a disposable one-night stand. After everything we'd been through together, how could you treat me exactly like all the rest?" She lifted her tearful gaze to his and spoke from the heart. "Why did you sleep with me?" she whispered. "Did you ever care for me at all?"

He stared at her.

"You were a convenience," he said roughly, turning away. "Nothing more."

The words felt like a knife blade in her heart, serrated, rusty, tearing through her flesh. She'd loved him with such devotion, and the night she'd given him her virginity, she'd thought a miracle had happened: that he'd fallen for her, too.

"Every woman in this city thinks she can tame you. The rich, handsome playboy," she choked out. She shook her head. "The truth is you'll never trust anyone long enough to care. You desert a woman the instant you've had your minute of cheap pleasure!"

Eduardo's eyes narrowed. Then his gaze traced slowly over her lips, her neck, her breasts.

"Longer than a minute, I assure you," he drawled. "Or don't you remember?"

Their eyes met, and her cheeks flooded with warmth. Heaven help her, but she remembered every hot, sensual detail of the night he'd made love to her. She still dreamed of it every night against her will. How he'd stroked her virginal body, how he'd peeled off her clothes and kissed every inch of her skin, how he'd made her scream with pleasure, crying out his name as he suckled her, as he licked her, as he filled her until she wept with mindless joy.

Heaven help her, but she couldn't forget.

His gaze dropped. Callie sucked in her breath when she realized the neckline of her tatty, oversize wedding dress had slid down her shoulder to reveal far too much of one plump breast and a full inch of her white cotton bra. She yanked the neckline up, scowling. "I can't believe I ever let you seduce me."

"Seduce?" His lips twisted with amusement. "What a charming description. I didn't seduce you. You jumped into my arms the instant I touched you. But call it *seduction*, if it makes your conscience easy."

She gasped in outrage. "You are such a—"

"Oh, I'm sure you regretted it afterward. McLinn must have taken it hard." He shook his head. "Amazing," he mused, "to think he was willing to marry you while you were pregnant by another man. He must be insanely in love with you."

A twinge of unease went through her. "He's not in love with me. He's my best friend."

"And you must have felt so guilty." Reaching over, he twirled a tendril of her brown hair. "So full of remorse that you ruined your chaste, loyal, boring love affair of years for a single night of hot, raw lust with me."

She jerked away. "You are so full of yourself to think—"

"Why did I treat you exactly like the rest? I'll tell you." Eduardo's eyes met hers evenly. "Because you are no different."

"I hate you!"

He snorted a laugh, but his eyes were icy. "Then we agree on something at last."

Tears fell down her lashes as she looked down, suddenly deflated. "All I wanted was to give my baby a good home," she whispered. "But now, instead of two loving parents, she'll be pulled like a tug-of-war rope between a mother and father who hate each other. Two parents who aren't even married. The world can be cruel. She'll be called *illegitimate*. She'll be called a bastard…"

Eduardo's eyes widened. "What?" he exploded.

"She'll always feel she's not good enough, as if she were some kind of accident, some kind of mistake. When the truth is you and I are the ones to blame." She looked up at him with a sob. "I don't want her to suffer. Please, Eduardo. Can't you just let me marry Brandon? For her sake?"

He looked at her for a long moment, his expression half-wild.

Then his jaw set. He abruptly leaned forward in his seat to say something in rapid-fire Spanish to his chauffeur then turned away, dialing into his phone and speaking again in the same language, too fast for her to understand. Praying she'd made him see reason, that he'd changed his mind and would let her go, she watched him, tracing the harsh lines of his silhouetted face, the handsome, sensual, cruel face she'd once loved with all her heart.

When Eduardo turned back to her, his dark eyes were strangely bright. "I have happy news for you, *querida*. You are going to be married today after all."

She let out a sob of joy. "You're taking me back to Brandon?"

He gave a hard laugh. "You think I would allow that?"

Callie frowned, confused. "But you just said—"

"You are going to be married today." Eduardo gave her a smile so icy cold it reminded her of the winter wind whipping across the empty, frozen prairie. "To me."

CHAPTER TWO

CALLIE gasped. Marry Eduardo? The father of her baby? Her ex-boss? The man she despised more than anyone on earth?

Shocked, she stared at him as she waited for the punch line. Licking her lips nervously, she finally said, "I don't get the joke."

Eduardo's lips curved humorlessly. "It's not a joke."

She spread her arms wide in the backseat of the car. "Of course it is!"

Eduardo grabbed her left hand, looking down at her cheap engagement ring with its microscopic diamond. "No, Callie, *that* is a joke."

Trying to rip her hand from his grasp, she glared at him. "A ring is a symbol of fidelity, no wonder you hate it!"

"You'll have a real one."

"I'm not going to marry you!"

"Oh, right. I forgot you're a *romantic*. I should ask you properly," he said sardonically. His dark eyes gleamed as he wrapped her hand in his own and pressed it against his chest. Before her horrified eyes, he went down on one knee in the back of the car. "*Querida*, my darling, my dear, will you do me the deep, deep honor of becoming my wife?"

She felt the heat of his hard chest through his suit, and her heart fluttered—even as her cheeks burned at the mockery in his voice. Anger gave her strength, and she jerked her hand from his grasp. "Go to hell!"

He moved back to his seat. "I'll take that as a yes."

Rain pattered against the roof of the car, horns honking around them as the car moved through traffic. The rain-splattered streets passed in a gray blur.

Callie realized Eduardo meant it.

He actually wanted her to be his wife.

"But you—you don't want to get married!" she stammered. "You've said as much to every woman you've dated. You practically had it tattooed on your chest!"

"I always planned to marry the mother of my children."

"Yes—but you wanted to marry some ritzy Spanish duchess!"

The edges of his lips lifted. "The best laid plans," he said. "You are having my child. We must wed."

He made it sound like a punishment—for him. She lifted her chin. "Gee, thanks," she said sarcastically. "I'm touched. Five minutes ago, you didn't even believe you were the father. You said you wouldn't believe a word I said. Now you want to marry me?"

"I've decided that not even you, Callie, would lie to me about our baby's paternity. Not when the truth is so clearly unpleasant to you."

She folded her arms, glaring at him. "I'm having your baby, all right, but nothing on earth could make me be your wife."

"Strange. You were keen to get married a few minutes ago."

"To Brandon!" she cried. "I adore him. I'd trust him with my life!"

"Spare me his list of virtues," Eduardo said, sounding bored. "Your love makes you blind."

"He might not be rich and heartless like you, but that's

exactly why he'll make a wonderful father. Far better than—"

She cut herself off as a painful contraction arced through her body.

"Far better than me?" Eduardo said with dangerous softness. "Because I am not good enough to be her father. And that was your excuse for lying to me and marrying your lover."

"He's not my lover—"

"Perhaps not physically. But you *love* him. So you were going to steal my child. And you accuse me of being heartless," he said contemptuously. "You are breathtaking."

The words were not a compliment.

Callie held her breath as new pain assailed her. Her baby wasn't due for two and a half weeks, but this was starting to feel very different from the Braxton-Hicks contractions she'd had last week. *Very* different.

Was it possible…?

Could it be…?

No! She forced herself to take a deep, calming breath. It couldn't be real labor. It was sixteen days too soon. Stress was causing her body to react, that was all. She had to calm down, for the baby's sake!

She shifted in the backseat of the car, trying to alleviate the stabbing pain in her lower back. "You don't want to raise a baby and you certainly don't want me as your wife. It's only your masculine pride that makes you—"

"My masculine pride." Eduardo bared his teeth into a smile. "Is that what you call it?"

"You don't want to marry me, I know you don't. You're just in shock. You haven't had time to think what it would mean for you to raise a child. To have a family."

"You think I've had no time to consider what it means

for a child to feel abandoned by his parents? To feel alone? To have no real home?"

Callie closed her mouth with a snap. Of course he knew. Licking her lips, she tried helplessly. "I could give our baby a wonderful home—"

"I know you will." His eyes were fathomless and stark. "Because I will provide that home. As her father."

There was no winning this war. Now that Eduardo knew about her pregnancy, he would never give up his rights as a father.

"So what do we do?" Callie said miserably.

"I told you. Marry."

"But I can't be your wife."

"Why?"

"I—I don't love you."

"Good," he bit out. "Your sainted McLinn can keep your love. Just your body and your vow of fidelity are enough."

Her heart was pounding in her throat. "You really want to marry me?" she whispered. The thought made her tremble. In spite of everything, she couldn't forget the romantic dreams she'd once had of Eduardo taking her in his arms and saying, *I made the worst mistake of my life when I let you go, Callie. I love you. Come back to me. Be mine— forever.* "As in forever?"

Eduardo gave an ugly laugh. "Be married to you forever? No. I have no desire to live the rest of my life in hell, chained to a woman I'll never be able to trust. Our marriage will last just long enough to give our child a name."

"Oh." She shifted in her seat then frowned. That changed things a bit. "Like—like a marriage of convenience?"

"Call it what you like."

"For a week or two?"

"Let us say three months. Long enough for it to actually

look like a real marriage. And for our baby's first months to be the best possible, with us both in the same home."

"But—where would we live? My lease is gone. You sold your brownstone in the Village."

"I just bought a place on the Upper West Side."

She blinked. "You were moving back to New York, because you thought I'd be gone."

His lips twisted. "I bought it as an investment. But you are correct."

Callie stared up at him, her heart pounding. "This is never going to work."

"It will."

She took a deep breath. *Marriage.* Would it be good for their baby, as Eduardo believed? Or would it only make their frayed relationship even worse, creating yet more accusations and distrust between them?

"But how would our marriage end?" she said. "With an ugly divorce—throwing plates and screaming at each other? That wouldn't help anyone, least of all my baby."

"*Our* baby," he corrected, then bared his teeth in a smile. "Our prenuptial agreement will outline our divorce. We will agree from the beginning how it will end."

"Plan our divorce before we're even wed? That seems so sad…."

"Not sad. Civilized." He lifted a dark eyebrow, rubbing the rough, dark edge of his jawline. He gave her a tight smile. "Since we are not in love, there will be no hard feelings when we part."

Three months. Callie swallowed. She tried to imagine what it would be like to live in Eduardo's house. Even as his secretary, she'd never lived with him on such intimate terms. And though she was no longer the naive, trusting girl who'd fallen in love with him so stupidly, he still had such frightening power over her. Callie's foolish, traitorous body yearned for him like a sugary, buttery cake that was impossibly bad for her but she couldn't stop craving just the same.

"And if I refuse?" she whispered. "If I get out of this car and flag a taxi back to Brandon?"

His expression cooled.

"If you are truly so selfish that you'd put your desire for love ahead of the best interests of our child, I will have no choice but to question your fitness as a mother, and challenge you for full custody." She started to protest, but he cut her off calmly. "I have limitless funds and the best law firm in the city at my disposal. You will lose."

She felt another contraction and this time, the pain was so deep and sustained that she closed her eyes, bracing her body against it as she panted, "You're threatening me?"

"I'm telling you how it will be."

"We're here, sir," Sanchez, the driver, said from the front seat, as he pulled the sedan to the curb.

Looking out her window, Callie saw the same courthouse where she'd gotten a marriage license yesterday with Brandon. The thought of deserting her best friend to marry Eduardo was insane. But she could either become Mrs. Eduardo Cruz for three months, living in the same household and sharing custody of their newborn, or she could possibly lose her child forever.

"And…afterward…" she said haltingly, "how would we arrange custody?"

Eduardo gave her a smile that didn't meet his eyes. "Once you show that our child means more to you than some lover, and that you are a reasonable and concerned parent, I am sure we can work something out." As Sanchez got out of the front seat and walked around to open the door, Eduardo's voice turned hard. "You have thirty seconds to decide."

Shivering, she stared at him with her hands wrapped over her belly. She felt her baby moving inside her, and she was desperate to protect her. She glared at him, feeling trapped and frightened and furious all at once. "You've left me no choice."

The door opened behind Eduardo.

"I knew you'd see reason," he said sardonically. Climbing out, he turned back, holding out his hand. "Come, my bride."

For an instant, Callie was afraid to touch him—afraid of what it did to her. But as he waited, she reluctantly put her hand in his own. His hard, hot palm pressed against her skin, his larger fingers intertwined around hers. As he pulled her from the car to the sidewalk, she looked up at his face, remembering the first time she'd touched his hand.

Callie Woodville? The powerful CEO of Cruz Oil had been visiting his outpost in the Bakken fields of North Dakota. Callie was the local office liaison, sent from the nearby town of Fern. He'd held out his hand, looking sleek and urbane in a black suit, with his helicopter still noisily winding down behind him. *I've heard you run the entire office here, and do the work of four people.* His sudden, gorgeous smile lit up his darkly handsome face. *I could use an assistant like you in New York.*

She'd looked into the warmth of his dark eyes. Dazzled, she'd taken his outstretched hand. And that had been it. The thunderbolt she'd always prayed for. She'd loved him from that first moment. How she'd loved him...

Now, with Eduardo's hand still wrapped around hers, Callie was barely aware of people rushing by them on the busy New York sidewalk. The two of them were connected like the moon and the sun, as stars and comets streaked around them in the vastness of space. The two of them. Just like always.

But his handsome face had changed over the last year. It was subtle. Perhaps no one else would have even noticed. But she saw the tighter set of his jaw. The deeper crinkle around his hard eyes. His high, angled cheekbones seemed chiseled out of stone, and so did his jawline, already dark with five o'clock shadow. At thirty-six, he was even more ruthless and powerful than she remembered. His masculine beauty was breathtaking. Looking up into his deep black eyes, Callie trembled. It would be too easy to fall under his spell again, and forget the way he demanded total devotion from others, while offering none in return.

Eduardo's expression darkened. Reaching down, he tucked a tendril of her wavy brown hair behind her ear. "You will be mine, Callie. Only mine."

A shudder went through her. She was helpless, lost in his gaze. Lost in his touch. Lost in her traitorous heart's memory of how, for years, she'd lived for him, only for him.

A cough behind her broke the spell, causing her to jump away. An unsmiling bald man in a plain blue suit stood behind her. She recognized John Bleekman, Eduardo's chief attorney.

"Hello, Miss Woodville," he said expressionlessly.

"Um. Hello," she said, wondering why he was there.

He turned to Eduardo, holding out a file. "I have it, sir."

Taking the file, Eduardo opened it and glanced over the papers for several minutes. "Good." He handed it to Callie. "Sign."

"What is it?"

"Our prenuptial agreement."

"What? So fast?"

"I had Bleekman start drawing up the draft after I spoke with your sister this morning."

"But you didn't even know if it was true about the baby—much less that you wanted to marry me!"

"I always like to be prepared for every possibility."

"Yes." She scowled. "To make sure you get your way."

"To mitigate risk." He pushed a fountain pen into her hand. "Sign it. And we'll go get our marriage license."

Callie looked through the thick stack of papers of the prenuptial agreement. She started to read the first paragraph. It would probably take an hour to read it all. Frowning, she thumbed through the pages uncertainly. She saw the amount of money he intended to give her as alimony and child support and looked up with a gasp. "Are you crazy? I don't want your money!"

"My child will grow up in a safe, secure, comfortable home. That means she must never worry about money. And neither can you." He set his jaw, watching her with visible annoyance as she turned back to page two and continued reading through the document. "Do you intend to read every single word?"

"Of course I do." Lifting her head, she glared at him, even as pedestrians jostled them on the sidewalk. "I know you, Eduardo. I know how you operate—"

Her voice choked off as another sharp pain hit her body, so intense her spine straightened as she nearly gasped aloud. The contractions were getting worse. Surely this wasn't Braxton-Hicks. She was in labor. Real labor. The baby was on her way. Callie put one hand over her belly and exhaled through her teeth.

"What's wrong?"

Eduardo's voice had changed. Trying to hide the pain rolling through her in waves, she looked up.

His handsome face was looking down at her with concern. He was worried about her. His dark eyes were warm, warm as they'd been during the time when she'd been his infallible secretary, when she'd been the one woman he needed, the only woman he trusted. Before they'd slept together in the happiest night of her life, and then she'd lost everything.

The intensity of his gaze caused her heart to twist in her chest. She could cope with his cold anger or cruel words, but not his concern. Not his kindness. A lump rose in her throat, and she suddenly had to fight tears.

"Nothing's wrong," she said. "I just want to get this over with." Gripping the pen, she turned to the pages marked with yellow tags and rapidly scrawled her signature. It was all she could do to keep the pen steady, with her knees shaking. She shoved both the signed prenuptial agreement and pen against Eduardo's chest, then turned away to focus on her breathing.

Breathe in, breathe out. She tried to let the pain go through her without fighting it or tensing her muscles, but it was impossible. *Stupid useless breathing classes!*

"You didn't read it," Eduardo said behind her, sounding almost bewildered. "That's not like you."

A policeman mounted on horseback came clopping in their direction, even as yellow taxis and large buses whizzed down the street, honking noisily. But all the moving colors of the busy world seemed to slide like water around her. She didn't answer.

Eduardo touched her shoulder, turning her around. "Callie," he said huskily. "What is it?"

She couldn't speak over the ache in her throat. She'd loved him, in spite of his faults. She'd thought she was his one indispensible woman. Until he'd discarded her. She couldn't let herself care for him. And she couldn't let herself believe, even for an instant, that he cared for her.

"I just hate you, that's all," she bit out, pulling away. Pain ebbed from her body, and she exhaled, forcing her shoulders to relax. "Let's just get this sham of a wedding over with."

Without waiting for him, she started walking up the steps toward the courthouse.

"Fine." When he caught up with her, the brief concern in his voice was gone. He strode ahead to open the door, and when she saw his face, it was hard and cold again. She was glad. She couldn't bear his tenderness, not in his eyes and not in his voice. Even after all this time, it twisted her heart into a million pieces.

Three months, she told herself, her teeth chattering. *Then I'll be free.*

She followed him into the courthouse, with his lawyer trailing behind. Twenty-two minutes later, they walked back out with the license. Callie knew it was exactly twenty-two minutes, because she'd started timing her contractions with her watch.

Eduardo didn't touch her as they walked down the steps. He didn't smile. He barely looked at her. After bidding the lawyer farewell, he led her toward the black car at the curb. "I have made arrangements for us to be married privately at my home," he said coolly, as if discussing a business arrangement. Which, Callie reminded herself savagely, was exactly what it was.

She tried to follow, desperate to get their nightmare wedding over and done with, but another contraction hit her. Panting, she grabbed his arm. "I don't think I can."

He looked at her, his eyes flinty. "It's too late for second thoughts."

Sun burst through the clouds as light rain fell, sprinkling against her hot skin. She felt the contraction build inside her, and she could no longer deny what was happening. She gripped his jacket sleeve tightly. "I think…I think I'm in labor."

He sucked in his breath, searching her gaze. "Labor?"

Wheezing, she nodded. As the pain built, her knees went weak beneath her and she felt herself start to collapse toward the sidewalk.

Then she felt Eduardo's strong arms around her as he lifted her against his chest. It felt good, so good, to be cradled in his arms that she nearly wept. He looked down at her, his jaw tight.

"How long?" he demanded.

Her body was starting to shake with the pain and she saw from his expression that he could feel it, too. "All... day...I—I think..."

"Damn you, Callie!" he said hoarsely. "Why do you hide everything?"

She was in too much agony to answer. His jaw clenched and he turned away, racing to the curb. "Sanchez! Door!" he shouted, and his driver sprang into action. Seconds later, she was in the backseat of the black sedan. Eduardo took her hands in his own as he asked urgently, "Which hospital, Callie? The name of your doctor?"

She told him, as Eduardo turned to shout the information at his driver, growling at him to drive faster, *faster*.

"Just hold on, *querida*," Eduardo said softly to her, stroking her hair. "We're almost there."

But Callie was lost in pain as the car flew down the streets of New York, taking sharp turns and honking wildly until the car sharply stopped. The car door flung open, and she was dimly aware of Eduardo shouting that his wife needed help, help *now* dammit!

"But I'm not your wife," Callie breathed as she was wheeled into the hospital. She looked up at him, blinking back tears even as the pain started to recede. "We only have a license. We're not married."

Callie heard him gasp before she was whisked away by

a nurse to a private examination room. As the contraction eased, she changed into a hospital gown. When the nurse came back through the door, Callie got a single glimpse of Eduardo pacing in the hallway, barking madly into a phone at his ear. Then the door closed, and the round-faced, smiling nurse came to check her. She straightened. "Six centimeters dilated. Oh, my goodness. This baby is on the way. We'll notify the doctor and get you to your room. I'm afraid it might be too late for anesthesia…"

"Don't—care—just want my baby to—be all right…" But before Callie had even been wheeled to her private labor and delivery room, the new contraction had already begun. Each one was worse than the last, and this one hit her so badly it made her whole body shake. Rising to her feet, reaching toward her bed, Callie covered her mouth as nausea suddenly roiled through her.

Quickly Eduardo came behind her. He snatched up the trash can and gave it to her just in time for her to be sick in it. Afterward, as the pain receded, Callie sat down on her hospital bed and cried. She cried from pain, from fear, and most of all from knowing that she'd just been vulner-able in front of Eduardo Cruz…and was about to be even more vulnerable.

But there was no way out now.

Only one way through.

"Help her!" Eduardo bit out at the nurse, who gave him an understanding smile.

"I'm sorry. I don't think there's time for meds. But don't worry. The doctor is on his way.…"

Eduardo snarled a curse that involved the doctor's lack-ing moral qualities, intelligence and bloodline. Growling, he went to the door and peered out into the hallway for the third time before Callie heard him mutter, "Thank God. What took so long?"

"All good things take time." A smiling, white-haired man in a suit followed him back into the private delivery suite. Eduardo went to Callie, who was stretched out across the hospital bed with her feet in stirrups, taking deep breaths and trying to relax before the next contraction.

"That's not my doctor!" she cried.

Eduardo knelt beside the bed. "He's going to marry us, Callie."

She looked between them in shock. "Right now?"

He gave her a crooked half smile, pushing sweaty tendrils of hair off her face. "Why? Are you busy?"

Callie looked at the trim man with the white beard and bow tie. "Is he authorized to just randomly marry people?"

The corners of his lips quirked. "He's a justice of the New York Supreme Court. So yes."

"There's a twenty-four-hour waiting period after the license—"

"He's waived it."

"And my previous license—"

"Handled."

"Everything always goes your way, doesn't it?" she grumbled.

Leaning over the hospital bed, he kissed her sweaty forehead. "No," he said in a low voice. "But this time it will." He turned back to the judge. "We are ready."

"The doctor will be here any second," the nurse warned.

"I'll do the express version, then." The judge stood in front of the beeping, flashing displays that monitored both Callie's heart rate and the baby's, and gave the plump nurse a wink. "Will you be my witness?"

"All right," the nurse said with a girlish blush. "But make it quick."

"Quicker 'n quick. So. We're gathered here in this hospital room to marry this man and this woman." The judge peered down at Callie's huge belly. "And none too soon, I'd say…"

"Just get on with it, Leland," Eduardo snapped.

"Do you, Eduardo Jorge Cruz, take this woman—what's your name, my dear?"

"It's Calliope," Eduardo answered for her through clenched teeth. "Calliope Marlena Woodville."

"Is it really?" The judge looked at her sympathetically through wire-rimmed glasses. "How very unfortunate for you."

"From my mother's—favorite soap opera," she panted.

"Right. So do you, Eduardo, take this woman, Calliope Marlena Woodville, to be your lawfully wedded wife?"

"I do."

Callie felt the pain starting to build again, and grabbed Eduardo's shirt. Looking at her, he put his hand over hers, then said angrily to the judge, "Hurry, damn you!"

"And do you, Calliope Woodville, promise to love Eduardo Jorge Cruz, forsaking all others, till death do you part?"

Eduardo looked down at her with his dark eyes. Once, this had been all Callie ever wanted, to promise her love and fidelity to him forever. And now it was happening. She was promising to love him forever, though she knew it was a lie.

It *was* a lie, wasn't it?

"Callie?" Eduardo said in a low voice.

"I do," she choked out.

Eduardo exhaled. Had he wondered, for a brief instant, if she might refuse? No, impossible. He was too arrogant, too sure of his control over women, to ever doubt….

"I see you already have the ring," the judge said, then blinked in surprise at the tiny diamond on Callie's hand.

"I must say, Eduardo," he murmured, "that's unusually restrained for you."

She was still wearing Brandon's engagement ring! Horrified, Callie tried to pull it off her swollen finger, but it was stuck. "I'm sorry—I…forgot…"

Without a word, Eduardo eased the ring from her finger and tossed it in the trash. "I will buy you a ring," he said flatly. "One worthy of my wife."

"Don't worry." She gave him a weak smile as she felt the pain start to build again. She panted, "Our marriage will be so short it really doesn't matter…"

"That's the spirit," the judge said jovially. "Ring can come later. Or not. Well, kids, we'll just skip through and assume the part about forsaking all others and staying together for better or worse. And since with Eduardo I already know it'll be for richer, not poorer, I reckon that's about it."

Callie stared at the judge, then Eduardo. The wedding ceremony had passed by in a flash. Just a few words spoken, and two lives—soon, three—forever changed. How could something so life-changing be so fast?

The judge gave them a big grin. "You may now kiss the bride."

She nearly gasped. *Kiss?* She'd forgotten that part! He was going to kiss her?

Eduardo turned to her. Their eyes met. He slowly leaned over the bed, and for an instant, all the pain fled Callie's body in a breathless flash.

When his mouth was an inch from hers, he hesitated. She could feel the warmth of his breath against her skin, causing prickles up and down the length of her body.

Then he lowered his lips to hers.

Eduardo kissed her, and prickles turned to spiraling electricity, sizzling her nerves like a current sparking up and down her body. His lips were hot and soft, in pledge of their promise, inflaming her senses from within. It lasted only a brief moment, but when he pulled away, Callie's hands were shaking, and not from pain.

"Congratulations, you crazy kids," the justice said, beaming at them. "You're married."

Married. Callie's body flashed cold over the magnitude of what she'd just done. She'd married Eduardo. She was his wife.

Just for three months, she reminded herself desperately. The prenuptial agreement had been clear about the timetable. At least in the paragraphs she'd skimmed before the contraction had hit her… She tensed as another contraction hit, burning through her like wildfire. She gasped, biting back a cry as her doctor came in, a brown-haired man in his late fifties. Glancing at the monitors, he checked her. Then he smiled. "Seems you're good at this, especially for a first-time mother. All right, Callie. Time to push."

Her eyes went wide as fear ripped through her. Instinctively she reached for Eduardo's hand, looking up at him with pleading eyes.

Eduardo took both her hands in his. "Callie, I'm here." His voice was deep and calm as his dark eyes looked straight into hers. "I'm right here."

Panting, she focused only on his black eyes, letting herself be drawn into them. As she started to push, bringing her baby into the world, she'd never felt any pain so deep. She gripped her new husband's hands so tightly she thought she'd break his bones, but Eduardo never flinched, not once. He never left her. As she held on to him for dear life, nurses moving around them at lightning speed, monitors beeping, she focused through her tears on his single, blurry image. Eduardo was her one solid, immovable focal point.

He never looked away.

He never backed down.

He never left her.

And in the end, the pain was worth it.

A healthy seven-pound-eight-ounce baby girl was finally placed in Callie's arms. She looked down at her daughter in amazement, at the sweetest weight she'd ever known. Cuddled against her chest, the baby blinked up at her sleepily.

Leaning over them, Eduardo kissed Callie's sweaty forehead, then their baby's. For a long, perfect moment, as medical personnel bustled around them, the newly married couple sat together on the bed with their brand-new baby.

"Thank you, Callie, for the greatest gift of my life," Eduardo said softly, stroking the baby's cheek. He looked up, and his dark, luminous eyes pierced her soul. "A family."

CHAPTER THREE

EDUARDO CRUZ had always known he'd have a family different from the one he'd grown up in. Different.

Better.

His home would have the joyous chaos of many children, instead of a lonely, solitary existence. His children would have comfort and security, with plenty of food and money. And most of all: his children would have two parents, neither of whom would be selfish enough to abandon their children.

The first time Eduardo had seen a truly happy family, he'd been ten, hungrily trolling the aisles of a tiny grocer's shop in his poor village in southern Spain. A gleaming black sedan had pulled up on the dusty road, and a wealthy, distinguished-looking man had entered the shop, followed by his wife and children. As the man asked the shopkeeper for directions to Madrid, Eduardo watched the beautifully dressed woman walk around with her two young children. When they clamored for ice cream, she didn't yell or slap them. Instead she'd hugged them, ruffled their hair then laughed with her husband as he'd pulled out his wallet with a sigh. Handing out the ice creams, the man had whispered something in his wife's ear as he wrapped his arm around her waist. Eduardo had watched as they left, getting back in their luxury car and disappearing down the road to their fairy-tale lives.

"Who was that?" Eduardo had breathed.

"The Duke and Duchess of Quixota. I recognize them from the papers," the elderly shopkeeper had replied, looking equally awed. Then he turned to Eduardo with a frown. "But what are you doing here? I told your parents they'd get no more credit. What's this?" Grabbing the neck of Eduardo's threadbare, too-short jacket, he pulled out the three ice cream bars melting in his pocket. "You're stealing?" he cried, his face harsh. "But I should have expected it, from a family like yours!"

Humiliated and ashamed, Eduardo's heart felt like it would burst, but his face was blank. At ten years old, he'd learned not to show his feelings from a mother who raged at him if he laughed, and a father who beat him if he cried.

Scowling, the shopkeeper held up the ice cream bars. "Why?"

Eduardo's stomach growled. There was no food at home, but that wasn't the reason. He'd been sent home from school early today for getting into a fight, but his father hadn't cared about what had caused the fight. He'd just hit Eduardo across the face and kicked him from the house. He was too disabled—and too drunk—to do anything but lie on the couch and rage against his faithless wife. Eduardo's mother, who worked as a barmaid in the next village, had been coming home less and less, and three days ago, she'd disappeared completely. The boys at school had taunted Eduardo. *Not even your mother thinks you're worth staying for.*

When he'd seen the *Madrileños* eating ice creams, Eduardo had had the confused thought that if he took some home, his family might love each other, too. *¡Idiota!*

Crushing, miserable fury filled him. He suddenly hated them—all of them.

"Well?" the grocer demanded.

"Keep it, then!" Reaching out a grubby hand, Eduardo knocked the ice cream bars to the floor. He'd turned and run out of the shop, running as fast as his legs could carry him, gasping as he ran for home.

And it was then he'd found his father…

Eduardo blinked. He looked around the comfort and luxury of his chauffeured, three-hundred-thousand-dollar car. His eyes were strangely wet as he looked down at his two-day-old baby, sleeping peacefully in her car seat as Sanchez drove them home from the hospital.

Her childhood would be different.

Different.

Better.

He'd never let the selfishness of adults destroy her innocent happiness. He would protect her at all costs. He would kill for her. Die for her. Do anything.

Even be married to her mother.

As the car drove north on Madison Avenue, Eduardo's eyes looked past the baby to Callie on the other side. He'd once thought she was the only person he could really trust, but the joke was on him.

She'd lied to his face for years.

And not just to him. A few hours after the birth, Callie had called her family to tell them about her new marriage and new baby. White-faced and trembling, she'd refused to speak to her sister then started crying as she spoke to her mother. When Eduardo had heard her father yelling on the other line, leaving Callie in tearful, pitiful sobs, he'd finally snatched the phone away. He'd intended to calm the man down. But it hadn't exactly turned out that way.

He scowled, remembering Walter Woodville's angry

words. Setting his jaw, Eduardo pushed the memory aside. The man was clearly a tyrant. No wonder Callie had learned to keep things to herself. His eyes narrowed.

Then he looked back at his sleeping daughter, and his heartbeat calmed. For the past two days he hadn't been able to stop staring at her tiny fingers. Her plump cheeks. Her long eyelashes. The way she unconsciously pursed her tiny mouth to suckle, even while she slept.

Eduardo took a deep breath.

He had a child. A family of his own.

He had a wife.

He'd married Callie to give their baby a name, he reminded himself, then he scowled. And yet she was still nameless.

He glared at his wife and bit out, "María."

Callie looked back sharply, her vivid green eyes glinting like emeralds sparkling in the sun. "I told you no. My baby will not be named after your Spanish dream wife. No way."

He exhaled, regretting he'd ever told his trusted secretary that he wished to marry María de Leondros, the young, beautiful Duchess of Alda. They'd only met socially once or twice, but marrying her would have been a satisfying way to prove how far he'd come since the days he'd stolen ice creams. "María is a common name," he said evenly. "It was my great-aunt's name."

"Bite me."

"You're being jealous for no reason. I never even slept with María de Leondros!"

"Lucky her." She folded her arms, glaring at him. "My daughter's name is Soleil."

Irritated, Eduardo set his jaw. Was it so strange that he wished to name his child after his Tía María, who'd brought him to New York, who'd worked three jobs to support him? María Cruz had encouraged him to see his high-school job pumping gas in Brooklyn not as a dead-end, but a place to begin. After she'd died, he'd gone from driving a gas truck, to owning a small gasoline distribution business, which he'd sold at twenty-four to become a wildcatter. His first big find had been in Alaska, followed by Oklahoma. Now Cruz Oil had drilling operations all over the world.

Yet Callie stubbornly refused to be reasonable. Instead she pushed for the name *Soleil,* which meant nothing personal to anyone—she'd just found it in a baby name book and liked the sound! He set his jaw. "You are being irrational."

"No, you are," she retorted. "You're already giving her a surname, and I chose her name months ago. I'm not changing it because of your whim."

He lifted his eyebrows incredulously. "My *whim*?"

"Soleil is pretty!"

"Did it, too, come from your mother's favorite *telenovela*?"

"Go to hell," she said, turning to stare out the window as they drove through the city. Silence fell in the backseat. Eduardo took a deep breath, clenching his hands into fists. His wife's stubbornness exceeded common sense! Because of her, they'd had to leave the hospital without yet filing a birth certificate.

His jaw set grimly, he turned back to her. "Callie—"

But her eyes were closed, her cheek pressed against the car window. He heard the rhythm of her breathing, and realized to his shock that she'd fallen asleep in the middle of their argument.

He looked at her beautiful face, against the backdrop of Central Park, the vivid green trees and lawn reminding him of her eyes. Her light brown hair fell in soft waves against her roses-and-cream complexion. As usual, she wore no makeup, but no ingénue on Broadway could hold a candle to her natural beauty. She wore the baggy knit pants and long-sleeved T-shirt his staff had brought to the hospital, but he knew the hidden curves of her generous figure would put any scrawny swimsuit model to shame.

For months he'd tried not to remember her beauty, but being this close to her, the reality overwhelmed him. His wife was the most desirable woman on earth. Even with those dark hollows beneath her eyes.

A sharp edge rose in his throat. Turning, he looked out at the brilliant dappled early evening light glowing gold through the trees. Callie had given birth to their child without anesthesia. He still couldn't comprehend that kind of bravery, that kind of strength. For the last two nights, as he'd slept in a chair beside her bed, Callie had barely slept at all. The baby had had some difficulty learning how to nurse, and Callie had been up almost every hour. He'd offered to help, and so had the nurses, but she'd insisted on doing everything herself. "She's my baby," Callie had whispered, her face pale with exhaustion. "She needs me."

Looking at Callie now, asleep with her face pressed against the window, Eduardo was forced to acknowledge feelings he'd never thought he'd feel for her again.

Admiration. Appreciation. *Respect*.

Things she'd clearly never felt for him.

"I've heard all about you, Eduardo Cruz." Walter Woodville had hissed over the phone two days ago. "Do you expect me to be grateful to you for doing the honorable thing and marrying my daughter?"

Eduardo knew Callie's family meant everything to her, so he'd contained his temper. "Mr. Woodville, I understand your feelings, but surely you can see…"

"Understand? Understand? You seduced my daughter. You used her and tossed her aside." Walter Woodville's voice was sodden with anger and grief. "And when you found out she was pregnant, you weren't even man enough to come and ask me for her hand. You just selfishly took her. *You stole my daughter.*"

Those particular words ripped through Eduardo like a blade. Then rage built through him in turn. "We never expected it to happen, but I have taken responsibility. I will provide for both Callie and the child—"

"*Responsibility,*" Walter spat out. "All you can offer is money. You might own half our town, but I know the kind of man you really are." The old man's voice caught, then hardened. "You'll never be a decent husband or father, and you know it. If you're even half a man, you'll send her and the baby home to people who are capable of loving them."

Then to Eduardo's shock, the man had hung up, leaving him standing in the hospital room, staring at his phone, wide-eyed with rage. No one spoke to him like that—well, no one except Callie.

But the old man wasn't afraid of him. He knew Eduardo's faults and flaws. And there could be only one person who'd told him.

Funny to think how he'd once trusted her. He'd wanted her in his bed almost from the start, but he'd needed Callie Woodville so much in his office, in his life, that he'd forbidden himself to ever act on his desire.

Until last Christmas Eve.

In a lavish, gilded ballroom of a Midtown hotel, Eduardo had found himself stone-cold sober at his own Christmas party, surrounded by Cruz Oil's vice presidents and board members and their trophy wives. The men in tuxedos, the women dripping diamonds and furs, had danced and drunk the spiked eggnog, alternatively boasting about the latest promising data in Colombia or gleefully discussing the expensive toys they planned to buy with their next stock bonuses.

Eduardo had watched them. He should have been in his element. Instead he'd felt lost. Disconnected.

He had everything he'd ever wanted. He controlled everything; he was vulnerable to no one. He'd thought being strong and powerful and rich would make him content, or at least, impervious to pain. Instead he just felt…alone.

Then he saw her on the other side of the ballroom.

Callie wore a simple, modest sheath dress. She stopped, her emerald eyes wide, and a flash went through him like fire.

In this cavernous ballroom, filled with tinsel and champagne and silvery lights, nothing was warm. Nothing was real. Nothing mattered.

Except her.

"Excuse me." Shoving his untasted glass of mulled wine into his CFO's hands, he'd walked straight through the crowd. Without a word, he'd taken Callie's hand. He'd pulled her out of the ballroom, and she didn't resist as he led her out into the white, icy winter night. Not waiting for his limo, he'd hailed a taxi to Bank Street, where he'd carried her to his bed. There, amid the breathless hush of midnight, he'd made love to her. He'd taken her virginity. He'd held her tight, so tight, as if she were a life raft that might save him from a devouring black sea.

He'd never felt anything like that night, before or since. Their passion had resulted in a baby.

It had resulted in a wife.

Eduardo's eyes narrowed as he looked at Callie, still sleeping as the car exited Central Park into the city streets of the exclusive Upper West Side.

You seduced my daughter, Walter Woodville had accused. The truth was that she had seduced Eduardo. With her innocence. With her warmth. With her fire.

But she was a liar. She'd hidden so much from him. He could never trust her again.

Only his baby mattered now. With her dark hair, she was his spitting image. Eduardo had known she was his child long before that morning's paternity test confirmed it. But if Sami Woodville hadn't called him two days ago out of the blue, his baby would be living in North Dakota right now. She'd be Brandon McLinn's daughter.

Eduardo's jaw clenched. Even if Callie was in love with another man, he could hardly believe she'd betrayed him so deeply. But he didn't have to trust her. He had a private investigator on staff who could tell him everything he needed to know about Callie. He'd never be fooled by her again.

He would keep his friends close, his enemies closer and his wife the closest of all.

The sedan arrived at his twenty-floor building on West End Avenue. As Sanchez opened the door, Eduardo carefully, breathlessly, lifted his sleeping baby out of the car seat. He walked slowly so he didn't wake her, cradling her head against his chest as the doorman held open the door. The baby was so tiny, he thought. So helpless and fragile. And he loved her. Love swelled his heart until it ached inside his ribs. He let himself love her as he'd never loved anyone.

His plump, gray-haired housekeeper, Mrs. McAuliffe, was waiting in the luxurious lobby. "The nursery is ready. Och, what a sweet babe!"

"Do you know how to hold a baby?" he demanded.

"Why, I'm insulted, Mr. Cruz! You know I raised four children of my own."

"Here." Gently he thrust the sleeping baby into her arms, watching anxiously. As the older woman cooed softly in admiration, Eduardo turned and raced back outside.

The September sun was still hot, pouring golden light through the white clouds. His driver was reaching for his wife's door when Eduardo stopped him. "I'll do it, Sanchez."

"Of course, sir."

Eduardo looked down at Callie through the car window. Her head had fallen back, her beautiful face now leaning against the leather seat. Dark, long eyelashes fluttered against her pale skin. She looked so young. So tired.

As he lifted her into his arms, she stirred but did not wake. Her eyelashes fluttered and she murmured something in her sleep, nestling her cheek against his chest as her wavy light brown hair fell back on his shoulder.

She weighed next to nothing, he thought. Looking down at his wife, his heart gave a strange thump. While Sanchez drove the car to the underground garage, Eduardo carried Callie inside. He took his private elevator to the top floor.

He'd closed on this two-story penthouse a week ago as an investment. The penthouse had been languishing on the market for two years with a thirty-six-million-dollar price tag before he'd bought it for a steal, at the fire sale price of twenty-seven million. He hadn't intended to live here for long. But now...his plans were rapidly changing.

"I'll take the baby to the nursery, sir," his housekeeper said softly when he came out of the elevator. He nodded then carried his wife across the large, two-story foyer with its Brazilian hardwood floor in a patterned mosaic. Going up the sweeping stairs, he started down the hall toward the guest room.

Then he stopped.

The master bedroom would be better for Callie in every way. It was larger, with a huge en suite bathroom and a wall of windows overlooking the city and the Hudson River. Most importantly, it was adjacent to the study, which had been turned into the nursery. Shifting Callie's weight in his arms, Eduardo turned back. Carrying her into his bedroom, he put her down on his king-size bed. *Sí.* It was better.

Callie shifted, murmuring in her sleep as she turned on his soft feather pillow with its thousand-thread-count Egyptian cotton pillowcase. Eduardo closed the heavy curtains around the windows, darkening the room. He covered her sleeping form with a blanket, then for a long moment, he looked down at her, listening to her steady, even breath.

He'd only meant their marriage to last three months. He hadn't thought he could endure it for longer.

But in the forty-eight hours since the birth, his perspective had changed.

His daughter was small and innocent and oh, so fragile. Eduardo knew what it meant to feel like unwanted baggage, like a stray without a home. He wanted his daughter to feel safe and protected, not split between divorced parents, between two lives. He wanted her to have not just a name, but a real home. A real family.

And no matter what Eduardo thought of Callie, he knew she loved their baby. He'd seen it in the way she'd fought through the pain of childbirth with such bravery. In the way she'd sacrificed her own body, her own sleep and peace, in order to nurture and cherish their child. Even in the way she'd fought with him over her name.

Eduardo's jaw set. If Callie could endure pain, so could he. He turned away. There would be no divorce. They both would sacrifice. He would give up his desire for a wife he could trust. She would give up her dreams of love. Love was an illusion, anyway.

Responsibility was not.

She might not like his plan. Eduardo exhaled, remembering her horrified reaction when he'd first proposed marriage. She wouldn't accept a permanent union without a fight. So he would give her time to accept their loveless marriage. To appreciate what he could offer. To forget the people she'd left behind.

His hand tightened on the doorknob. He'd give her the agreed-upon three months to see the benefits of their marriage. And if, at the end, Callie still wanted her freedom?

He glanced back through the shadowy bedroom with narrowed eyes. Then he'd ruthlessly keep her prisoner, like a songbird in a gilded cage. Walking into the hallway, Eduardo shut the double doors behind him with quiet, ominous finality.

Now that Callie was his wife, he never intended to let her go.

CHAPTER FOUR

CALLIE sat up straight in bed.

Disoriented, she put her hands to her head, feeling dizzy and half-asleep as she looked around the strange, dark room. Where was she? How did she get in this bed? Her breasts were full and aching, and she was still dressed in the same long-sleeved T-shirt and knit pants she'd worn from the hospital. She had no memory of how she'd gotten here, but she'd thought she heard her baby crying....

Her baby! She sucked in her breath. Where was her baby?

"Soleil?" she whimpered. She jumped up from bed and screamed, "Soleil!"

Light flooded the room from the hallway as double doors opened. Suddenly Eduardo's arms were around her.

"Where is she?" she cried in panic, struggling in his arms. She looked up at the hard lines of his face, half-hidden in shadows. "Where have you taken her?"

"She's here." Eduardo abruptly released her, crossing the bedroom to fling open a door. "Here!"

Her baby's cries became louder. With a gasp, Callie ran through the door. As he turned on a lamp, she saw the bassinet. Sobbing with relief, she scooped her baby up into her arms.

The baby's cries subsided the instant she was cradled

against her mother's breast, but she was clearly hungry. Callie sat down in a soft glider near the lamp and started to pull up her T-shirt. She stopped, looking up awkwardly at Eduardo. "I need to feed her."

His dark eyes shimmered in the dim lamplight. "Go ahead."

"You're watching."

"I've seen your breasts before."

She glared at him. "Turn around!"

He lifted an eyebrow then with a sigh he turned away.

Once he was safely facing the other direction, Callie lifted up her shirt, pulled down her nursing bra and got her baby latched on to her breast. She flinched at first then relaxed as her tiny daughter started gulping blissfully.

"Sounds like she was hungry."

"Don't listen!" Callie cried, annoyed.

He gave a low laugh. "Sorry."

Moments passed in silence, and Callie took a deep breath, suddenly ashamed. "I'm sorry about earlier. I just panicked. I woke up in a strange place and didn't know where I was."

His spine stiffened, but he didn't turn. "You fell asleep in the car, on the way home. I carried you upstairs. Don't you remember?"

The last thing she recalled was arguing with him as they drove through Central Park. He'd been pressuring her about their baby's name—as if Callie would ever name her sweet newborn after a spoiled Spanish heiress! But the soft hum of the engine had been hypnotic.

"I guess I was tired." She rubbed her hand over her eyes. "I slept so hard that I almost thought you'd drugged me so you could steal the baby. Funny, right?"

His voice was cold. "Hilarious."

"I'm sorry," she whispered. "I didn't mean to accuse you of…" Her throat constricted.

He turned to face her, but he definitely wasn't looking at her breasts. "Of stealing the baby?"

She swallowed. "Yes."

His eyes glimmered in the dim light. "Don't worry about it."

He was being nice, which made her feel even worse. For months, she'd hated Eduardo, calling him a coldhearted jerk to her parents and friends, telling them stories about his worst flaws, telling herself he didn't deserve to be a father.

But *she* was the coldhearted jerk. Her lips parted. If not for Sami's meddling, she would have done the dreadful thing she'd just accused him of: she'd have stolen their baby. He never would have even known he had a daughter.

How could Eduardo stand to look at her?

"I was wrong not to tell you." It took all her courage to meet his eyes. "I'm so sorry. Can you ever forgive me?"

"Forget it," he said harshly. He folded his arms. "We both made mistakes. It's in the past. Our marriage is a fresh start."

"Thank you," she whispered, feeling like she didn't deserve his generosity. Awkwardly she looked around them. The nursery was straight out of a celebrity magazine, with soft yellow walls, stuffed animals, and the sleek comfort of an expensive designer crib and bassinet. "This is nice."

"I had my staff redecorate the study while we were at the hospital."

"Your staff?"

"Mrs. McAuliffe."

"I've always known I liked her," Callie said with a

smile, trying to lighten the mood. "So next door is the guest room?"

He shook his head. "It's the master bedroom."

Her heart plummeted. "I…I was sleeping in your bed?"

"*Sí.*"

"Oh." She swallowed and tried to pretend it was no big deal that she'd slept sprawled across the same bed where Eduardo Cruz slept naked every night, when he wasn't entertaining lingerie models. Feeling self-conscious, she moved her baby to the other breast, quickly covering up any flash of skin with her cotton shirt. Cheeks flaming, she glanced up at Eduardo, but thank heaven, he was carefully looking away. "Well, thanks," she said with forced cheerfulness. "I'll move to the guest room later."

"You will stay in the master bedroom," he said evenly, "close to our baby."

"Then where would you sleep?" A sudden dreadful thought struck her. "You surely can't think you and I will—"

He cut her off. "I will take the guest room."

"I don't want to inconvenience you."

"You won't." Coming forward, he touched the infant's soft, downy head. "I want you to be here. Both of you."

Looking up at him, she breathed, "You—you do?"

"Of course I do." Eduardo looked at her, and his dark eyes cut straight through her heart. "I've dreamed of having a family like this. Of keeping them safe and warm. Protecting them." He squared his shoulders. "And I will."

The cold, ruthless edges of his expression had melted away, changing to something warm, something fiercely tender. He looked like another man, she thought in wonder. The man he might have been if his childhood had been less of a tragedy.

Compassion mixed with longing and the echoes of her love, rising in her heart. But she couldn't let it win. She wouldn't. She took a deep breath. "Thanks for taking such good care of me." With a trembling smile, she looked down at the baby falling asleep in her arms. "And Soleil."

"Marisol," he said abruptly.

She blinked. "What?"

"Marisol. It's a classic Spanish name. A blend of your favorite name—Soleil—and my aunt's name. María."

Callie licked her lips. "Marisol," she tried. She didn't hate it. She tried again, "Marisol…Cruz."

"Marisol Samantha Cruz," he said softly.

She looked up, her eyes wide with shock. "After my sister?"

"She brought our family together."

"Sami betrayed me!"

"She's family. You will forgive her." He looked down at her. "We both know you will."

Callie stared at him in consternation. No. No way! She'd never forgive her sister for going behind her back and telling Eduardo about the baby—never!

And yet…

How could she be angry at Sami for betraying her, when telling Eduardo the truth had been the right thing to do? Even if Sami's motives hadn't been totally pure. A tremble went through Callie. Even if her sister's motivation had only been because she was in love with Brandon.

Sami was in love with Brandon. Callie had to face it. For years, she'd seen the way Sami hung on Brandon's every word, but she'd told herself it couldn't possibly be serious. Her sister had a crush. Puppy love. Callie hadn't seen the truth. She doubted Brandon did, either. They'd never noticed Sami's devoted, anguished love, right in front of their very eyes.

But Brandon deserved to be loved like that, as every husband wanted to be loved by his wife. Callie had been selfish to accept his proposal, to think, even for an instant, that friendship would be enough for a marriage. How could she have even thought of allowing him to make that sacrifice? A sob escaped her throat. She'd very nearly ruined so many lives.

Looking down, Eduardo put his hand gently on her shoulder.

"I've heard you talk about your little sister for years," he said quietly. "You send her gifts, write her letters. You're putting her through college. We both know you're going to forgive her."

Callie looked up at him, blinking back tears. "You're right," she whispered. "I was so angry at her. But she didn't do anything wrong." She closed her eyes. "It was all me."

Silence fell. When she opened her eyes, Eduardo's forehead was furrowed, as if he couldn't understand her. Their eyes met, and she felt that strange tugging at her heart. With an intake of breath, she turned away. "Fine."

"Fine?"

"Her middle name can be Samantha." Callie touched her baby's plump, soft cheek. "Marisol Samantha Cruz."

"I don't believe it." A ghost of a smile lifted the corners of Eduardo's lips. "Are we in agreement? I can fill out the birth certificate?"

Looking up at him, she smiled back. "Yup."

"Wonders never cease." For a long moment, their eyes met in the soft light of the nursery, with their baby slumbering between them. Then clearing his throat, he glanced at his platinum watch. "It's nearly ten. You must be starving."

"Not really…" As if on cue, her stomach growled. "I guess I am."

"I'll make you something."

"You? You'll cook?" she said faintly.

She must have sounded dubious, because Eduardo smiled. "I am not completely helpless."

"You must have changed a lot in the last nine months. The man I knew could barely find his own kitchen." She shook her head with a snort. "I'm amazed you even survived without me."

He looked at her.

"It wasn't easy," he said gruffly. Turning, he paused at the door. "Come down when you are ready."

Callie stared at the empty doorway, bewildered at this friendlier mood between them. Looking down at her sleeping newborn, she rocked back and forth in the soft cushioned glider, cuddling her close. She gazed in wonder at her downy dark hair. Her daughter had Callie's snub little nose and round face, with her father's dark coloring and olive-colored skin. She would be a beauty. How could she not be, with such a father?

In all the years Callie worked for Eduardo, she'd never once seen him put someone else's comfort above his own. But in the last two days, he'd asked her to marry him. He'd slept in a chair for two nights at the hospital. He'd brought her to his home. Turned his study into a nursery. He'd given Callie his bed while he himself was relegated to the guest room down the hall. He'd asked her to teach him how to swaddle their baby and change her tiny, doll-size diapers. Coldhearted billionaire tycoon Eduardo Cruz, changing a baby's diaper? That was something she'd never imagined in a million years!

It won't last, Callie told herself fiercely. When the novelty wore off, Eduardo would chafe at the responsibility and intimacy of family. He would crave the freedom of sixteen-hour workdays and endless one-night stands. He would return to the selfish, cold playboy he was at heart. Very soon—likely before the three months was even up—

he would divorce Callie, and be relieved to make his parental support of Marisol the distant, financial kind.

Once that happened, Callie and her baby would go back to North Dakota. To her family. To the people who loved her.

Or did they?

She swallowed. Her phone call to her family, just hours after the birth when she was still exhausted and in pain, had officially been a disaster. Callie tried to explain that she'd just had a baby and gotten married to a man they didn't know except by reputation, and planned to live in New York for the foreseeable future. Her mother had just sobbed as if her heart was breaking. As for her father...

Her shoulders tightened. Her father never reacted well when his wife was crying. But he'd never spoken to Callie like that before—as if she were such a disappointment he didn't even want to call her his daughter. As if he yearned to disown her.

An ache filled her throat. She'd never planned to get pregnant, but keeping her baby a secret had just made it a million times worse. And that phone call had changed something between them. She felt estranged from her family, and it was like half her heart was missing.

But she also felt angry. How could her family have turned on her like this? They were supposed to love her. Why couldn't they see her side?

And her father had been so harsh to Eduardo. Callie still didn't know exactly what he'd said. She just remembered how Eduardo's expression had changed when they were talking on the phone, from conciliation to cold fury.

Walter Woodville had never liked the way Cruz Oil had swept into their town, bulldozing through the county with money and influence, luring young people from family farms with the promise of high-paying jobs. But Callie had made that initial dislike worse. Her cheeks burned as she recalled her bitter words about Eduardo after he'd fired her. Was it any wonder that stalwart, old-fashioned Walter, who'd married his high school sweetheart and still farmed land once owned by his grandfather, had been horrified by the idea of such a man knocking up his daughter, and worse—marrying her?

And as for Brandon…

Her cheeks reddened further with shame and regret. Brandon was certainly back in North Dakota by now, after driving across the country alone. She wondered what he'd told her parents. What he felt inside. Was he worried about her? Was he angry? Or worse—brokenhearted?

Amazing to think he was willing to marry you while you were pregnant by another man. He must be insanely in love with you.

Callie shook Eduardo's words away. Brandon wasn't in love with her. Friends just tried to help each other. But no—that was a cop-out. She swallowed. He'd been kind, and she'd taken advantage. She needed to call him and beg for forgiveness.

Another person she'd hurt. She slowly rose to her feet, her body sore, her legs shaking with exhaustion. As she tucked her sleeping daughter into the bassinet, she suddenly remembered the tender light in Eduardo's dark eyes when he'd held Marisol for the first time. Remembered how he'd dozed on a chair in their hospital room, cuddling their daughter against his naked chest so the baby could feel the warmth and comfort of skin on skin. Strange. In this moment, she felt closer to Eduardo than anyone else. Eduardo.

Creeping softly out of the nursery, she went to the bedroom, where she found the suitcase of new clothes his staff had brought to the hospital. Opening it on the enormous bed, she selected a pink cashmere lounge set and sighed. It probably cost the equivalent of a week's salary. But the cashmere felt soft.

Taking a hot shower in the marble en suite bathroom was pure heaven. After combing her wet hair, Callie put on the soft cashmere set over a white cotton t-shirt and went downstairs.

It wasn't just a penthouse, she thought in amazement. It was a mansion in the sky. She went down the sweeping stairs to the great room, with a fireplace and floor-to-ceiling windows that showed the sparkling lights of New York City by night.

"What do you think?"

She jumped and turned. Eduardo walked toward her with two martini glasses. He was wearing dark jeans and a black T-shirt that showed off his exquisitely muscled body. "It's incredible," she breathed. "Like nothing else I've seen."

"Good." He gave her a slow-rising smile. "I'm glad you like it, since it's yours." She blushed, but still couldn't look away from his powerful body, or the masculine beauty of his face. *Hers.* If only that were true!

He held out an orange-filled martini glass. "Here."

"I can't drink while I'm nursing."

He held up his own drink, a clear martini with an olive. "This is mine." He pushed the orange-colored drink into her hand. "This is juice."

"Oh. Thanks," she said, suddenly realizing she was dying of thirst. She drank it all in one swallow, then wiped her mouth and realized she was hungry, too. "Something smells delicious from the kitchen," she said hopefully, setting down her glass.

Eduardo was staring at her. "I made quesadillas and rice."

"Great!"

"You might not like them." He smiled again, but for the first time she noticed that his smile didn't reach his eyes. His hand was gripping the stem of his martini glass, his shoulders tense. "Like you said, I'm helpless in the kitchen. Not like some men, who are undoubtedly born chefs."

Callie frowned, puzzled at his sudden change in mood. "Is something wrong?"

He showed his teeth in something like a smile. "Not a thing."

"You just seem—strange."

"I'm fine. Shall we have dinner?"

"Sure," she said reluctantly. Maybe she was so tired she was starting to imagine things. Or maybe it was her guilt talking. With a sigh, she looked around. "Have you seen my purse? I just need to make a quick call."

"Your family?"

"No," she said, irritated at the suggestion. "I called them from the hospital and look where it got me. No. Brandon."

Eduardo's dark eyes flashed in the shadowy room. "No."

"He must be back in Fern by now. I'm sure he's worried about me, and I'm worried about him—"

"He's fine," Eduardo said coolly. He finished off his martini and placed the empty glass on the marble mantel. "I just spoke with him."

She stared at him. "You did?"

"He'd been calling for hours. I got sick of the phone ringing. Ten minutes ago, I answered the phone and told him to stop."

"What did he say?"

"An earful," he said grimly. He set his jaw. "What exactly did you tell him about me?"

Her cheeks grew hot. "I was angry after you fired me. I might have called you a world-class jerk."

"A jerk?"

"And a workaholic with no heart, who lures a new woman into bed each night, only to put her out with the trash each morning," she whispered. She shook her head. "I'm sorry. I shouldn't have said it."

Eduardo gave her a hard smile. "You just told him the truth." Reaching for his empty martini glass, he pulled the olive off the toothpick with his white teeth and slowly chewed. "I am all of those things. Just as you are secretive, naive and ridiculously sentimental."

Protestations rose to Callie's lips then faded. After the way she'd acted, how could she argue with that—any of it?

He came closer, his face silhouetted by the huge windows that sparkled with the lights of the city. "But we must endure it."

"Endure it?" she whispered.

"Each other," he said coldly. "For Marisol's sake."

Pain cracked through her heart. Just a moment before, she'd been filled with hope. But now she saw she really was alone. No one was on her side. No one.

Stiffening, she held out her hand. "Give me my phone."

"No."

"Fine," she bit out. "I'll find it myself."

Moving through the swinging door, she went into a large, luxurious kitchen, with top-of-the-line appliances, a wine fridge, and a pizza oven, overlooking the sparkle of the city and black void of the Hudson River. Her eyes widened as she saw her bag on a granite countertop. She snatched it up, digging all the way to the bottom.

"It's not in there," Eduardo said, watching her.

Still digging, she didn't bother to look up. "Where is it?"

"I threw it away."

Her hand stilled. "Are you kidding me?"

His voice was like ice. "I won't let you call him."

"You can't stop me!" Her eyes were wide as she gasped with outraged fury. "You had no right!"

"I'm your husband. I had every right."

"I'll get a new phone!"

His black eyes glittered. "Try it."

"This is ridiculous. I'm not your prisoner!"

"For as long as we are married, I expect your loyalty."

"He's my best friend!"

"And you are my wife."

"You can't possibly feel threatened by—"

"No, why would I?" His voice was low and full of dislike. "Just because he is the man you *adore*, the man you *trust*, the man you wanted to be Marisol's father. The man you tried to marry two days ago."

"Only because I was pregnant—"

"You were engaged *years* ago, Callie," he snapped. "Before I even met you!"

Her mouth fell open. "What?"

Eduardo leaned his hand on the kitchen countertop. "Last Christmas Eve, when we made love," he ground out, "I couldn't sleep with you in my bed—"

"So why didn't you kick me out?"

He ground his teeth. "I went for a walk. I decided to stop at your apartment to collect a few of your things. I was going to ask you to stay. I never expected to find a man living there with you."

"You—what?"

His jaw was hard as he shook his head. "After our years together, I'd actually thought I could trust you. But just hours after you gave me your virginity, I met your live-in love. Your longtime fiancé."

She gaped at him.

"What, no witty comeback?" he jibed.

"Brandon wasn't my fiancé. Not back then!"

His eyes grew wild. "Stop it, damn you! Will you never stop lying? *I met him!*"

"But we only got engaged a few weeks ago!"

Eduardo folded his arms, his expression as hard as the wooden floors. "Then how do you explain it? Either you are lying, or he was. Which is it?"

She licked her lips. "Brandon wouldn't lie," she said weakly. "Unless—" She covered her mouth with her hand.

If we're not married by thirty—Brandon had taken her hands in his own—*let's marry each other.*

Sure, she'd laughed. On the night of their senior prom, thirty had seemed a million miles away. *Why not?*

She'd thought it was a joke. But could Brandon have taken it seriously? Could that be why, the day after Eduardo had gotten her an apartment, Brandon had suddenly shown up in New York with no job and a suitcase full of jeans? Because he'd heard in Callie's voice that she was falling completely in love with her boss, and wanted to protect his territory?

No. It couldn't be. Brandon loved her as a friend. Just a friend!

She glared at Eduardo. "Either you misunderstood him, or Brandon was trying to warn you off. To protect me from a sleazy boss."

"Sleazy?" he gasped.

She folded her arms. "But there's never been anything romantic between Brandon and me. Let me call him and prove it!"

"He's in love with you." His eyes were like ice. "You're either lying, or blind. But I won't be played for a fool ever again. You will not communicate with McLinn in any way.

Not by phone, by computer or via carrier pigeon. And not through your parents. Do you understand?"

Callie couldn't believe he was being so unreasonable. Tears rose to her eyes. "But I just left him there," she whispered. "Standing in the street on our wedding day. He deserves an explanation!"

"He saw you leave with me. That is all the explanation he needs. And if not…" He allowed himself a cold smile. "I just told him everything he needs to know."

A chill went down her spine. "What did you say to him?"

Turning away, he scooped up quesadillas and rice on a plate and shoved it toward her on the countertop. "It's simple. Contact him during our marriage, just once, and you are in breach of our agreement."

"Fine, I'll be in breach! Keep your stupid alimony. I don't care about your money!"

"Do you care about custody?"

She sucked in her breath. "What?"

He lifted an eyebrow. "It seems you did not read our prenuptial agreement very carefully before you signed it."

She struggled to remember the words of the prenup, but the truth was she'd barely skimmed the first pages. "I was in labor! In pain, under duress! Whatever I may have signed, it will never stand up in court!"

He gave her grim smile. "Shall we find out?"

Callie couldn't believe he could be so heartless. No, on second thought, she could. What she couldn't believe was her own stupidity—in believing it was possible for Eduardo Cruz to be anything *but* heartless! Blinking back tears, she tried to keep her voice from trembling. "Just let me talk to him once. You can listen on the other line. I just need to tell him I'm sorry." She closed her eyes. "When I think of what I did to him…"

"Yes, I can only imagine how badly you feel," Eduardo said sardonically. "Knowing you caused him pain by flinging yourself enthusiastically into bed with me and conceiving my child instead of his. A pity raising Marisol is now a responsibility more important than the romantic longings of your heart!"

His sardonic tone tore at her soul like nails on a chalkboard. "Why do you even care?" she spat out. "Our marriage will be over in months. For that matter, why did you even marry me? Why make such a song and dance about giving our child a name and a father and a home, when we both know you'll never last for long?"

His hand tightened into a fist on the counter. "What are you talking about?"

"I know you too well," she said. "I know the life you love. Traveling around the world, beating your competitors, buying expensive toys you barely take time to enjoy, any more than the women whose names you can't remember. Keeping score with your billions in the bank." She lifted her chin. "Am I leaving anything out?"

His dark eyes were cold. "My priorities have changed."

"For how long? A few days? A week? How long will you last before you abandon us?"

"*Abandon*?" he ground out. "You mean, how long until I let you rush into another man's arms?"

She shook her head. "I'm sick of your stupid jealousy!"

"And I'm sick of constantly being told it's impossible for me to be a decent husband, oh, no, not like some unemployed farmer who hangs on your every word. Too bad for you he's not Marisol's father!"

It was the last straw.

"Yes, it is!" Callie cried, blinking back tears. Grabbing her plate of quesadillas and rice—which indeed looked very poorly cooked—she yanked violently through the cupboards until she found a fork, then stomped across the kitchen. Stopping at the swinging door, she turned and yelled, "Three months can't come soon enough!"

Then with a sob, she ran upstairs, where she could eat and cry in peace with the one person in this world who still loved her—her baby.

CHAPTER FIVE

Three months later

IT HAD been a horrible three months of watching Eduardo be a perfect, loving, devoted father to their baby, who'd gone from tiny newborn to chubby baby who slept better through the night. Three months of being treated with distant courtesy as his wife. Three months of being tortured with memories, of silent hurt and anger and repressed longing by day—and haunted dreams at night. Three months.

Over.

Looking at herself in the bedroom mirror, Callie zipped up her silver dress, a slinky, strapless gown with a sweetheart neckline that emphasized her bustline. She put on the three-carat diamond stud earrings that matched the ten-carat diamond ring on her hand. Leaning forward, she applied mascara and red lipstick. Stepping back into crystal-studded high heels, she straightened. She stared at her own unsmiling image.

It was like looking at a stranger.

Callie thought of herself as plain and plump but the mirror now plainly told her otherwise. Her light brown hair was long and lustrous, blown-dry straight twice a week at the best salon on the Upper West Side. Her arms and legs had become toned and sleek from carrying Marisol and taking her on long autumn walks. She went to the park almost every day, rain or shine, eager to escape the penthouse, where she felt useless, trapped in the same house as a husband who did not care for her.

But her transformation into his trophy wife was complete. She no longer looked the part of the farm girl, or even the secretary. She was Mrs. Eduardo Cruz. The oil tycoon's unloved wife.

But tomorrow morning, her three-month marriage sentence would be over. She and her baby would be free.

Callie's green eyes were pools of misery.

Every night, she'd slept alone in his big bed as he slept in the guest room down the hall. Every day when Eduardo came home from work—earlier than he ever had, before dinner—his face lit up with joy as he scooped Marisol up in his arms. At night, when the baby couldn't sleep, she heard him walking the halls, cuddling her against his chest, singing her to sleep in his low baritone. Callie had a million new memories that would always twist her heart, because after they divorced, she'd never see them again.

Eduardo had been unfailingly courteous. He'd never brought up Brandon, her family, or any other subject that might cause an argument. Instead, every night as she sat beside him at the dinner table, he read the paper over dinner and kept the discussion to small talk. And her gaze unwillingly traced the sensual curve of his lips and shape of his hands, her body electrified with awareness as she breathed in his masculine scent and felt his warmth.

He never touched her. All he expected of Callie was for her to take care of their child and occasionally accompany him to charitable events. As they were doing tonight.

In the intimate world of New York society, the official Christmas season was kicked off in early December by the annual Winter Ball, which raised money for children's charities across the five boroughs. Tonight was the last night Callie would wear an elegant gown and accompany Eduardo in his dashing tuxedo. The last night she'd have to look up at her husband and pretend her heart wasn't breaking.

Tonight was the end.

Fitting that their marriage would end at a Christmas party, she thought dully. Just as it had begun with one. Tomorrow, as outlined by the prenuptial agreement, she would move out and Eduardo would begin divorce proceedings.

Standing in front of her bedroom mirror, Callie exhaled. She didn't believe for a single second that he'd been faithful to her. She knew him too well. He wasn't the type of man who could go without physical release for a month, much less three. He must have had lovers since their marriage—but where? How? It tortured her.

She put a trembling hand to her forehead. What did she care? Tomorrow, she'd be packing for North Dakota. For home. She missed her family. Sami. Her mother. Brandon. Even her father. She'd missed so much. Harvest. Autumn. Apple dunking and hot mulled cider. Thanksgiving with her father carving the turkey and her mother's prize-winning pumpkin pie. But she'd been resentful and angry. She'd wanted them to call and apologize. They had the number. But they hadn't called, and neither had she.

But tomorrow, she'd go home. She'd noted the date in her planner and circled it with a black pen. This sham marriage would be over.

No doubt Eduardo, too, had been watching the calendar. He'd done a wonderful job as a father but he must be exhausted, hiding his love affairs, working only nine hours a day instead of his usual sixteen, eating dinner at home every night. Honestly, she'd never expected him to last this long.

Callie shivered as if she felt the cold December wind blowing through the canyons of the city.

He'd never tried to touch her during their marriage, not once. They'd only had that single night together, the night they'd conceived Marisol. One perfect night, the fulfillment of all her innocent dreams. One night. And so much she would never forget. The sudden hot hunger of his gaze across the hotel ballroom. The warmth of his sensual lips as they kissed in the back of a taxi heading south on Fifth at a breakneck pace. The woodsy, clean scent of his black hair as he carried her up the stairs to his bedroom and how silky it had felt clutched in her fingers as he covered her naked body with his own. The low rasp of his breath as he cupped her breasts. His hard gasp as he pushed inside her. The sound of her own scream ringing in her ears as her world exploded like fireworks, like a million dreams coming true at once.

Tomorrow, she'd go home and try to find a regular job. She'd face her family. She'd forget Eduardo. She had to; otherwise the rest of her life would be bleak…

"*Querida*."

She whirled around. Eduardo was standing in the open doorway of the master bedroom, wearing a well-cut black tuxedo. He looked so devastatingly handsome that her heart lifted to her throat.

His eyes were as black as his jacket. His dark, short, wavy hair set off his handsome, chiseled face to perfection. As he came into the bedroom, the muscles of his powerful body seemed barely constrained by the civilized, sophisticated tuxedo.

He slowly looked her up and down, and his eyes seemed to devour her in the floor-length silver dress. "You look ridiculously beautiful," he said huskily. "Every man will envy me tonight."

"Oh," she said in shock, and blushed. She had no idea how to react. He'd never said such a thing to her before. On this, the last night of their marriage, she suddenly felt as awkward and self-conscious as if they were on a first date. "Thank you. Um. You, too."

He smiled. "I brought you a gift."

Pulling a black velvet box from his tuxedo pocket, he opened it in front of her. Her jaw dropped when she saw the priceless emerald and diamond necklace sparkling inside.

She looked up with a gasp. "That's—that's for me? Why?"

He gave a low laugh. "Do you really need to ask?"

She bit her lip. "Is it like—a going-away present?"

"No." He shook his head then gave her a charming, crooked grin. "Think of it as an early Christmas present." Setting down the box on the bed, he pulled the necklace from the black velvet setting. "May I?"

Nervously she held up her long brown hair and allowed him to place the necklace's heavy weight around her neck and latch it in the back, shivering as she felt his strong, warm hands brush against her nape. It was the first time he'd touched her in months, and it caused a tremble to rise from deep inside her. Moving away, she glanced at herself in the mirror. She put her hand over the green jewels sparkling in the light from the black wrought-iron chandelier.

"It's beautiful," she said over the lump in her throat.

Their eyes met in the mirror. The smile left his face.

"Not half as beautiful as you," he said in a low voice. "No other woman can compare."

He was standing behind her, so close their bodies could almost touch. Sensual need suddenly poured through her, so intense and deep that it made her knees weak. She closed her eyes.

"Why are you being nice to me?" she choked out. "Why now? When it's the end?"

Coming behind her, he put his hands on her bare shoulders. "Who says it's the end?"

She felt the weight of his hands on her skin and breathed, "The prenuptial agreement."

Eduardo turned her around, and she opened her eyes. She could feel the heat radiating from his body. Feel its answering, unwilling fire in her own.

Nervously she licked her lips. His gaze fell hungrily to her mouth. "You have to know what I want," he said softly.

His freedom, she thought unhappily. While as for her... The time of their marriage had only taught her to crave him again. To yearn. To want.

"Of course I know," she said, and tried to laugh. "It must have felt like the longest three months of your life."

He stroked her cheek. "It has."

She swallowed. "Three months of waiting, and waiting..."

"Three months of hell," he agreed.

She exhaled, blinking back tears as all her worst fears were proven true. "Well, tonight it will end."

His dark eyes tracing her face, her cheeks, her lips. "Yes," he said softly. "It will."

Shaking, she turned away, picking up her satin clutch off the bed. "I'm ready."

"Good." His sensual mouth curved as he held out his arm. "Mrs. Cruz."

Breathlessly she took his arm. He led her downstairs to the penthouse foyer, where they bid farewell to Mrs. McAuliffe, who would watch their sleeping baby. Eduardo pulled Callie's white fur wrap from the closet and placed it gently around her. She felt the weight of his hands against her shoulders and shivered, remembering last night's dream that had felt so real, when she'd imagined his naked body over hers. With a tremble, she glanced down at his thick fingers spread across the white faux fur. Heat flashed across her body as she remembered the sensation of his fingertips against her skin. Shuddering, she pulled away as they took the elevator downstairs and went outside.

"Good evening, Mr. Cruz, Mrs. Cruz," the smiling doorman said, tipping his cap. "Have a wonderful night."

"Thank you, Bernard." Eduardo put his hand on the small of Callie's back, guiding her to the black limo waiting at the curb. Sanchez held open the door as she climbed into the backseat, exhaling as she pulled away. And yet, as they drove through the sparkling, snowy city, every inch of her body was aware of her husband beside her. She didn't relax until the car stopped, and she could escape the tight space beside him.

The Winter Ball was being held at a glamorous old hotel on the edge of Central Park. As Callie walked through the lobby on her husband's arm, her fingers barely touching his sleeve, she looked up at the soaring, frescoed ceilings in awe. Cruz Oil's Christmas party last year had been huge, but it was nothing compared to this, the most lavish social event of the season. As they entered the enormous ballroom, she saw a winter wonderland. White twinkling lights sparkled from black bare trees, in front of a white background illuminated with pale lavender light. Winter was Callie's favorite season, December her favorite month, and she gasped with wonder at the fairy forest of white.

Then the fantasy came crashing down as she saw the guests milling around them: gorgeous, skinny social-ites and powerful men, the type who'd all gone to prep schools and Ivy League colleges, who'd come from the best families and summered together in Kennebunkport and Martha's Vineyard. And who was she? Nobody.

Back at the penthouse, Callie had felt pretty; but here, she felt chubby and awkward. Scrawny, tall models seemed to circle them like sharks, looking hungrily at Eduardo.

"Do you know them?" she whispered, clutching his arm as he led her past them through the crowd.

"Who?"

"Those women who are staring at you."

He glanced over at the gorgeous supermodels. "No."

"Oh." She swallowed. Was he telling the truth? Or just trying to spare her feelings? She felt an ache in her throat, wondering if he'd had affairs with any of them. If he hadn't, he was probably counting down the moments until their divorce, marking out his future sexual conquests. And who could blame him? Three months without sex would be was a long time for a man like Eduardo.

But not for her. Callie had only had one sexual experience in her whole life. And with the only man she'd ever wanted. She'd tried not to care, told herself their marriage was just a sham. But just the thought of him jumping into bed with any one of those gorgeous, hard-eyed women made her want to throw up.

But Eduardo wasn't looking at the models. He was looking at Callie. "Can I get you a drink?"

Nervously she nodded, and when Eduardo brought her a cup of punch in a crystal glass, she gulped it down.

"Be careful with that," he said, sounding amused as he sipped his own Hendrick's martini, garnished with a slice of cucumber. "It's stronger than you think."

But Callie was tired of being careful. The punch tasted fruity and tart and sweet, with a little bit of bite. It tasted like temptation. Finishing it off, she held out her glass. "Please get me another."

He shook his head, looking down at her with dark eyes. "Take care, *querida*."

"I'm tired of taking care," she whispered. "Just for this one night, I want to be reckless."

Eduardo gave her a slow grin. "As you wish."

Turning, he went toward the bar. When he returned, the intensity of his gaze flooded her with heat.

"Here," he said in a low voice, holding out her drink. Their fingers brushed as she took the glass, and she shivered.

For weeks, he'd treated her with distant civility. She might as well have been one of his staff, the nanny who cared for his child. But tonight... Tonight he was looking at her. Really *looking* at her. As if he wanted to rip off her dress, kiss every inch of her skin, and make her lose her mind with pleasure.

He left me, she reminded herself fiercely. *I mean nothing to him. He only slept with me in the first place because I was* convenient.

"Thanks," she muttered, taking the glass. "What's this drink called, anyway?"

His lips quirked. "It's called a Rudolph."

"A Rudolph? Why?"

"It'll make your nose red and you fly all night."

"Oh," she muttered. Ask a silly question. Knocking back her head, she drank deeply, aware of his gaze upon her face, her neck, her breasts. She kept drinking until the cup was empty, and she had no choice but to meet his eyes. His dark eyes caressed her face.

"Have you ever had a hangover before?"

"No."

"Want one?"

She'd never experienced a hangover, but the idea of waking up with one tomorrow sounded appealing. It would be a welcome distraction from their impending divorce. "Maybe."

Music from the orchestra swelled across the ballroom and he held out his hand. "Dance with me."

Shaking her head, she looked toward the gorgeous cluster of supermodel-types on the edge of the dance floor, who were still watching Eduardo with voracious eyes. "Why don't you ask one of them?"

He frowned at her then glanced over before setting his jaw. "Why would I?"

"They seem to know you."

"Lots of people know me."

A lump rose in her throat. "Why don't we just end the charade? You don't need to be so discreet. I know perfectly well that you've had lovers during our marriage."

His eyes turned sharp. "Who told you that?"

"No one had to tell me. We haven't been having sex, so I assumed…"

"You assumed wrong."

For a long moment, they stared at each other.

"Are you really telling me the truth?" she whispered, her heart in her throat. "But it's impossible. There must have been someone else!"

His dark eyes burned like fire. "So that is what you think of me." His voice was low and terse beneath the rising music. "That while insisting on your absolute fidelity, I would cheat on you and betray our marriage vows?"

"What else do you expect me to believe? I know you, Eduardo. There's no way you've been celibate for the last three months, especially when women throw themselves at you! No man could resist that. Especially not—"

"Especially not me?" he said with dangerous quietness.

She shook her head tearfully. "You got what you wanted. Our baby has your name. Now all your friends have seen me, they'll know you did the right thing by our baby, and they'll know why our marriage didn't last."

"Which is?"

"Just look at me!" Starting to feel dizzy from the alcohol and the heat of the ballroom, she looked down at her overflowing curves in the tight dress then gestured toward him. "And look at you!"

Eduardo's brow creased as he looked down at his tuxedo, then back at Callie in her silver gown—the gown that had made her feel so pretty at the house but that now only seemed to emphasize her overblown figure compared to the stick figures of the models. He shook his head. "I don't understand."

"Oh, forget it!" she choked out. "It doesn't matter. Not anymore!"

But as she started to leave, she felt his larger hand enfold her own. Taking the empty glass from her, he set it on the silver tray of a passing waiter and pulled her into his arms. His dark eyes searched hers. "I never betrayed you, Callie."

She licked her suddenly dry lips. "Why would you be faithful to me?"

"If you have to ask, you don't know me at all." His hand tightened on hers. "Dance with me."

Callie stared up at him, her heart in her throat. She knew she should refuse. Her mind was reeling at the thought that he'd been faithful to her. Without her anger, she was vulnerable. She had nothing to defend her. The marriage would end tomorrow. She was so close to being free. She couldn't let him any closer now. She should run, as fast and hard as she could.

But as he led her to the dance floor, she couldn't resist, any more than she could resist breathing.

"All right," she whispered. "Just once." *To say good-bye*, she told herself.

Turning to her, Eduardo pulled her against his body. All around them, pale purple shadows moved against soft lavender lights, and the white bare trees looked like lacy latticework beneath twinkling white stars. Surrounded by couples swaying to music, they began to dance. Eduardo held her tightly, nestling her against the white shirt of his tuxedo. She felt his warmth. His heat. She felt the strength of his arms around her.

Callie closed her eyes, pressing her face against his chest. She felt strangely safe. Protected. She felt as if she'd gone back in time, to that one perfect night when she'd felt he cared.

For the next two hours, they never left the dance floor, and Callie was lost in the haze of a perfect, romantic dream. As Eduardo held her, as she swayed in her silver gown, she looked up into his handsome, sensual face and everything else fell away. She barely heard the music. She and Eduardo were alone, in an enchanted winter forest.

And she realized she loved him.

She'd never stopped loving him.

Callie froze, staring up at him as unseen couples whirled around them in the violet shadows.

"What is it, *querida*?" Eduardo said softly, looking down at her.

Callie licked her lips, feeling dizzy and hot all over. She couldn't let herself love him again. She couldn't be that stupid. She couldn't.

"What are you trying to do to me?" she said hoarsely. "What are you doing?"

Eduardo stood still on the dance floor, looking down at her. A tremble went through her as a current of awareness sizzled down her veins. Her mouth felt suddenly dry as he stroked her cheek.

"What am I doing?" His dark eyes searched hers, and he whispered, "I'm kissing you."

Callie couldn't move, couldn't breathe, as he lowered his mouth to hers.

She felt the heat of his sensual lips like satin and the warmth of his breath in an embrace that swirled around her body with breathless magic. She felt his hard, hungry lips against her own. Felt the scratchy roughness of his chin, as his hands ran softly through her hair, then down the bare skin of her back.

His kiss was exactly how she remembered. Exactly how a kiss should be. His deeply passionate embrace didn't just promise pleasure—it whispered of eternity. And against her will, words filled her soul that were an incantation in her heart.

I love you, Eduardo.

I never stopped loving you.

Oh, God. Could he feel it on her lips as he kissed her? Had her own body betrayed her?

"I want you, Callie," he murmured against her skin.

She saw the blatant desire in his dark eyes and suddenly felt like crying.

"How can you torture me like this," she whispered, "when we both know in the morning you'll only toss me aside? I gave you my devotion. And you treated me like trash!"

"Callie!"

"No!" She ripped away, not wanting him to see the anguish in her eyes. She couldn't bear that final humiliation. Turning, she ran off the dance floor. Pushing through the crowd, she rushed through the ballroom, running past the coat check without stopping for her wrap. She ran blindly through the lobby and out of the hotel, into the street, where she was nearly run over. A taxi driver honked and yelled at her angrily, but she barely heard him. She crossed the street to Central Park.

The park looked almost eerie in its snowy whiteness beneath the black, bare trees, just like the illusion inside the ballroom, but dangerous and cold, the real thing.

Moonlight filled the dark sky, illuminating the small clouds around it, making them glow like pearls in black velvet. As Callie ran, she wept, and it wasn't soft, feminine weeping, but big gulping sobs. Wiping her eyes, she glanced behind her.

And saw Eduardo following, an ominous figure in black.

She gasped and started to run, tripping on her shoes as she ran deeper into the park. She raced headlong down the windswept path, knowing that if he caught up with her, he would see her shameful love for him and he'd see her pathetically broken heart.

One of the high-heeled shoes fell off her feet. Turning around, she started to go back for it, but when she saw him right behind her, she kicked off her other shoe instead and turned back to run. The frozen, snow-kissed path felt like cold knives against her bare feet, the silver dress dragged against her legs and the winter air bit against her naked shoulders.

Then Eduardo caught up with her. His powerful arms lifted her off the frozen ground.

"Go away." Crying, totally humiliated, she struggled against his hard chest. "Just leave me alone!"

"You think you're disposable to me?" he said grimly, looking down at her. The moonlight gave his black hair a silver halo, like a sensual, dark angel come to lure her to hell. "Is that what you think?"

"I know it!"

"You just had my baby," he ground out, his dark eyes glinting. "I'm not a brute. I wasn't going to force myself on you!"

She tried to kick her way free. "Of course not, when you have half the supermodels of this city queued up outside our door. How can I ever compete with that? You said it yourself—you can't wait to divorce me!"

"Oh, my God." His jaw clenched. "Do you know how much I've wanted you? How long? Do you?" he thundered.

She stared at him, shocked at his fury.

His voice dropped. "I've wanted you for a year, Callie. And I've waited for you. For a year."

"No," she whispered. "It's not true."

What she saw in his dark eyes made her shiver all over. "My God. How can you not know? How have you not seen it?"

Her heart nearly stopped in her chest. She licked her dry lips. "You haven't tried to touch me, not once. You've barely even looked at me."

"You were a new mother. You were drowning." Reaching out, he brushed long brown tendrils off her shoulders. "You didn't need me trying to seduce you, placing more demands on you when you were only getting four hours of sleep. You didn't need a lover. You needed a partner. You needed me to be a good father."

She stared at him.

"And you were," she choked out tearfully. "The best father Marisol could ever have had."

Callie heard his intake of breath, felt the way his hands tightened on her as he held her against his chest. Looking down at her, his angled face was in dark silhouette.

"Thank you," he said softly. All around them, the winter landscape glowed in the moonlight.

"You really—wanted me?" she whispered.

He gave a harsh laugh. "I tried not to. Told myself that our night together was meaningless. Reminded myself that you were a liar engaged to another man, and you'd betrayed us both when you gave me your virginity."

Ice flashed through her. "I—"

"But I couldn't forget you. No matter how I tried." He shifted her weight against his chest. "There has been no other woman since the night you were in my bed," he said roughly, looking down at her. "Do you understand what I am telling you? No other woman."

She stared at him. "But…but it's been a year."

His dark eyes looked through hers. "Yes."

Callie couldn't believe what she was hearing. She licked her lips. "But those pictures of you with that duchess in Spain…"

"She is beautiful," he whispered. He shook his head. "But she left me cold."

Tears spilled unheeded down Callie's cheeks, freezing against her skin as she looked up at her husband. "No. No, it can't be true. You can't have been celibate for a year, wanting me—"

"You don't believe me?" he said grimly. He released her, slowly letting her slide down his body to her feet. "Then believe this."

And lowering his head, he pulled her body roughly against his, and kissed her once more, hot and hard.

CHAPTER SIX

CALLIE'S mouth parted in a gasp as she felt the smooth satin of his lips, the sweet rough fire of his tongue. She felt the warm strength of his arms around her, and in the dark, cold solitude of Central Park, surrounded by snow and the bare black trees of winter, she felt an explosion of heat.

Murmuring words in Spanish, Eduardo tightened his embrace as he held her against his chest. She dimly felt the icy wind against her cheek as tendrils of her light brown hair blew all around them, but the sensation of his lips against hers felt like a thousand flickers of fire.

As he kissed her, a sigh escaped her lips and she tilted her head back to deepen the embrace. Feeling his body so strong and hard against hers, her endless longing could no longer be repressed. With a soft moan, she wrapped her arms around his neck. She no longer felt the cold air against her skin, the frigid ground beneath her feet. She barely heard the distant traffic of the city and the wind through the bare trees. The night was frozen and dark, but Callie felt hot as a summer's day, lit up from within.

Eduardo's hands stroked her back, down her bare arms. Prickles of need spiraled through her everywhere he touched. Everywhere he *didn't* touch.

His lips gentled against hers, seducing and enticing where they'd once demanded and taken. Memories of another winter night went through Callie, leaving her lost in time, as if all the grief and pain of the last year hadn't happened, and she'd teleported back into the most perfect night of her life.

She wrapped her fingers in his hair. He felt so good, so powerful and masculine. His warrior's body made her feel feminine and small, and as he kissed her, as his sensual mouth moved against hers, she was completely beneath his control....

Then, with a harsh intake of breath, Eduardo pulled away. Taking his phone from his pants pocket, he dialed. "Sanchez," he panted, never looking away from Callie. "Outside. At the corner."

Hanging up, he put the phone in his pocket and reached for her, lifting her back into his arms.

"You don't need to carry me," she whispered. "I'm not cold."

He looked down at her almost pleadingly. "Let me."

Exhaling, she relaxed into the warmth of his arms, and Eduardo carried her back down the path, stopping to pick up each of her shoes, holding Callie with one arm as if she weighed nothing at all. When they reached Central Park South, he put the high-heeled shoes on her feet and gently set her down on the sidewalk.

"Thank you," she said, shivering, but not from cold.

Without a word, he pulled off his black tuxedo jacket and wrapped it around her bare shoulders and sparkling silver dress. His eyes were dark, his voice deep. "Never thank me. It is what I want to do. Take care of you."

Callie swallowed, her mouth dry, her heart pounding as she leaned against him. Thick snowflakes, illuminated by streetlights, started to fall from the dark sky. Was it really possible that Eduardo had been celibate for a year, longing for her? That he'd known the same feelings she had… The lonely bed, the regret, and most of all: the end-less craving…?

Her mind told her it was impossible, but his kiss had told her differently.

"Callie," he whispered. "You know what I'm going to do to you when we get home."

Her heartbeat went crazy, her breathing became quick and shallow and she felt a little dizzy. He wanted her. She wanted him. But the last time he'd made love to her, the joy and heartbreak had nearly killed her. Their marriage was ending in just a few hours. She was so close to being free…

But suddenly, freedom from Eduardo sounded like death. Wrapping her arms around him, she placed her cheek against his white tuxedo shirt and closed her eyes, listening to the beat of his heart. They remained there, holding each other silently, as the soft snowflakes fell in their hair and tangled in their eyelashes.

"The car's here." His voice was hoarse. She opened her eyes and he led her into the backseat of the limo. As Sanchez drove them from the curb, Eduardo didn't seem to care who might see as he turned to her. Reaching out his hands, he cupped her face. He lowered his head to-ward hers.

At the last instant before their lips touched, she turned her head away. "I can't."

"Can't?" he said hoarsely. "Why? Because—because you love someone else?"

She looked at him in the backseat of the car. His face was so impossibly handsome that her heart twisted in her chest. Every inch of her body was crying out to be in his arms, but lifting her chin, she forced herself to say, "I'm afraid."

He blinked. "Afraid?"

Afraid it will rip my heart apart so thoroughly that the

pieces will never be glued back together. "I'm afraid…it wasn't part of our deal." She swallowed. "Our marriage is in name only."

Eduardo's sensual lips curved. "What gave you that idea?"

"At the courthouse, when we got the marriage license, you said—"

"*You* called it a marriage of convenience. Which it is. But I never said it would be a marriage in name only. I promised to remain faithful, and I have. But I cannot suffer, wanting you, for the rest of my life."

"You don't have to. Tomorrow is our three-month anniversary. Our marriage is over." She paused, suddenly confused by the look in his eyes. "Isn't it?"

"No." His eyes glittered in the Christmas lights as they drove through the city. "There will be no divorce."

Time seemed to stop for Callie.

Behind his head, she dimly saw the bright lights illuminating the colorful displays in shop windows. "But you said three months!"

"I changed my mind." He scowled at her. "From the day I held our baby, I knew that whatever I'd once planned, our marriage would be—must be—permanent. That is the best way to raise our child. The only way. I'd hoped you would come to realize that."

"But you said you'd divorce me," she whispered. The will-o'-the-wisp Christmas lights seemed to be dancing away, disappearing along with her dreams of returning home to her family. "You promised. You said our marriage was just to make our child legitimate, to give her your name!"

His eyes had turned utterly cold, his body taut beneath his tuxedo. "You should be pleased," he said stiffly. "As my wife, you have everything you could possibly want. A fortune at your disposal, beautiful homes, servants, clothes and jewels."

"But what about…" Her throat closed and she looked away. "What about the people I love?"

"You'll love your children," he ground out.

Wide-eyed, she turned back to face him. "Children?" she stammered. "As in…more than one?"

He narrowed his eyes. "It is lonely to be an only child. Marisol needs siblings. Sisters to play with. Brothers to protect her."

Callie stared at him, remembering what she'd heard about Eduardo's poverty-stricken childhood in Spain, about his mother who'd run off with her lover, and his proud, humiliated father, who'd shot himself in the aftermath with an old World War II rifle. At ten years old, Eduardo had been shipped off to a great-aunt he'd never met in New York, and even she had died when he was eighteen. He had no one. He was alone.

She couldn't even imagine it. As much as the restrictive rules of her old-fashioned parents had chafed her, and as much as her little sister had irritated her on a regular basis, Callie couldn't imagine being an only child—and an orphan to boot, whose parents had both chosen to abandon her. Sympathy choked her, but then she hardened her heart. "So just like that, you expect me to agree? You expect us to remain married, to have more children? To plan it all in such a cold-blooded fashion?"

Glaring at her, he sat back in the car seat, folding his arms. "Marisol will be wanted. She will be safe and loved. She will have two parents and a home. There will be no divorce."

Horrified, Callie stared at him.

Stay Eduardo's wife?

Forever?

Her heart twisted in her chest. It was all like some strange dream. For a moment she was mesmerized by his certainty. Perhaps Eduardo was right. Perhaps it would be better for Marisol…better for everyone.

But how could she stay married to him, loving him as she did? He still wanted to be married to her for one reason only: to give their child a good home. How could Callie spend the rest of her life giving him her love, when all he wanted was—at most—her body?

Could she sacrifice her heart, and all hope of ever being loved? Could she spend the rest of her life feeling unloved and alone, in order to give her child the home she deserved?

Swallowing, Callie lifted her chin. "My family would have to be part of Marisol's life. And mine. I miss them. My parents and my sister and—" She cut herself off, but too late.

A sneer rose to his lips. "And Brandon McLinn, of course. His light still glows so brightly in your heart." He set his jaw, turning away. "You disappoint me."

Controlling herself with a deep breath, she didn't rise to his bait. "It was unreasonable of you to block me from seeing him. The only reason I went along with your demand was because I knew that as soon as the three months was over I could—"

"Yes." His eyes were hard as he glared at her. "I know exactly what you were planning to do."

The limousine stopped and Sanchez opened the door. Miserably she followed Eduardo out of the car. Why did he always take things so wrong? Why did he persist in being jealous of Brandon?

Eduardo didn't even look at her as they walked through the lobby of their building. The hot passion of Central Park seemed to have evaporated like smoke. He pressed the button, and they stood without touching, waiting silently in front of the private elevator.

Then he abruptly turned to face her, his hands clenched.

"I've left you alone too long," he ground out, his eyes dark. "I was trying to give you space to grieve the past and accept your new life. To embrace your future as my wife." Furiously he seized her in his arms. "But I see I took the wrong path with you. I should have staked my claim long ago."

Callie stared up at him, her eyes wide with shock. "You can't—"

Tightening his grip on her, he brought his mouth down on hers in a hard, punishing kiss. Trembling, she tried to push him away, but he was too strong for her. Especially when his lips tasted like sweet fire...

The door to the elevator opened with a *ding*, and Eduardo lifted her up into his arms. He looked down at her fiercely.

"Tonight, wife," he growled, "I'm taking back my bed."

The elevator door hadn't even closed before he was pressing her against the mirrored wall, his mouth hard and hungry against hers. Callie had given up any thought of resisting. In fact, she'd given up any thought altogether. Wrapping her arms around his neck, she returned his kiss with equal hunger. He released her, letting her body slide down his, and she felt his hard desire for her. She felt hot, wearing his tuxedo jacket, and through the thin cotton of his shirt, she felt the strength and heat of his body as he held her tight and kissed her, so long and hard and deep that she prayed he'd never let her go.

At the *ding* of the elevator, he picked her up and carried her wordlessly through their massive foyer, beneath the crystals of the shadowy chandelier above. His black eyes never left hers as he carried her up the curved, sweeping staircase. His gaze reached into her heart, taking brutal possession of her soul.

"Och, you're home early!" Downstairs, Mrs. McAuliffe came out into the foyer, her voice cheerful. "The baby's sleeping and happy and—oh."

As if from a distance, Callie heard the woman's shocked intake of breath, saw her turn and flee back down the shadowy hall toward her own rooms on the first floor. But for once in her life, Callie wasn't embarrassed. She couldn't care. All that mattered was this.

Without a word, Eduardo carried her up the last stairs and down the hall to the master bedroom. He set her down on her feet beside the king-size bed. She glanced down at the mattress, remembering how she'd slept alone for all the nights of their marriage. But she would not be alone tonight.

Her husband caressed her hair, tucking tendrils behind her ear. She shivered as his rough fingertips brushed her sensitive earlobe, and his hand slowly moved down her cheek to her throat, beneath the expensive diamond-and-emerald necklace to the sensitive corner between her neck and shoulder. His body towered over hers as he pulled his oversize tuxedo jacket off her shoulders, dropping it to the floor.

Walking around her slowly, he stroked the bare skin of her shoulders. Fire raced up and down her body as he finally faced her, cupping her face. He lowered his mouth to hers.

His lips were soft and warm, rough and hard all at once, searing through her body like lava, melting her core from within. Her full breasts ached, crushed against his muscled chest. He reached around her, and she heard, and felt, the pull of the zipper. Suddenly the weight of the silver strapless gown fell to the hardwood floor.

Stepping back, Eduardo looked at her in the moonlight. "You're beautiful," he said hoarsely. "I've waited for you so long. Too long…"

Yanking off his black tie, he tossed it to the floor. But as he started to unbutton his tuxedo shirt, his hands seemed clumsy. She looked at his fingers and realized they were shaking, just as hers were. With a low curse, he finally just ripped off his shirt, popping the buttons with brute force and kicking the expensive garment away. She nearly gasped at the beauty of his incredible upper body in the moonlight. The muscles of his chest were hard and defined, from his broad shoulders to his nipples and the dark arrow of hair that traveled down his flat, hard belly.

Wearing only trousers, he came closer, running his fingers along the curve from her waist to her hip. His gaze devoured her in the plunging strapless bra and matching panties. Beneath his gaze, she should have been acutely aware of her body's every flaw, and yet she saw the hunger in his eyes and she'd never felt more womanly or desirable.

A low growl escaped Eduardo's lips. Grabbing her hips with both his hands, he pulled her to the bed. Sitting down on the edge, he lifted her into his lap, so she straddled him.

Wrapping his hands in her hair, he pulled her head down and kissed her fiercely. She kissed him back with equal force, gasping at the sensation when her naked belly brushed against his bare chest. He cupped her breasts over her silky strapless bra. Her nipples tightened to agonizing points, her breasts heavy and tight. Reaching around her with one hand, he unhooked her bra. His first sight of her full breasts, swollen to twice their normal size from nursing, made him gasp. He slowly reached to cup her bare skin. His large, rough hands caressed her naked breasts and Callie's body went tight, as a hot current of electricity traveled from her nipples to her toes, sending spirals of hot, aching need to her deepest core.

"So beautiful," he breathed again. The bed was covered in a pool of silvery light, leaving the two of them in their own magic world as he pushed her back against the pillows.

Never taking his gaze from hers, he stood beside the wall of windows overlooking the entire Upper West Side, and removed first his trousers, giving her a glance of his powerful legs and trunklike thighs, then his silk boxers.

Callie's heart lifted to her throat as her husband stood before her, utterly naked and unashamed.

The moonlight frosted his naked chest, giving him an otherworldly appearance, like a powerful warlord from the mists of legend, a fierce barbarian king. He looked dark, handsome and powerful, illuminated by a gleam of silver. He looked like a dark knight from a fantasy. He moved toward her, and her whole body—down to her soul—trembled from within. And in the magical silvery light, his erection jutted from his body, proud and hard and every bit as huge as she'd remembered.

A spasm of fear went through her. After childbirth, what if it hurt to have him inside her? What if he was rough? What if he even tried to be gentle but was still just so big that he split her apart?

Eduardo moved over her on the bed. She sucked in her breath as he stroked her cheek, slowly kissing down her neck. She tilted back her head as she felt his lips caress her skin, gasping as she felt his hands' featherlike touch, cupping her breasts. Lowering his head, he kissed one breast, then the other, and slowly stroked down her body, down her collarbone, down the soft curve of her belly. Tension coiled low and deep inside her, and hardly knowing what she was saying, she breathed, "Yes…"

"You're mine, Callie. Only mine." He put his hand on her cheek, his eyes dark. "Tell me…"

"I'm yours," she whispered, her voice choking on a sob. *Of course* she was his. She'd been his from the moment he'd first taken her hand, when he was the CEO of a global multibillion-dollar company and she was just his secretary.

Lowering his mouth to hers, he kissed her, long and deep. His tongue teased hers, lightly at first, then plunging deeper into her mouth as their tongues intertwined, slick and hot and wet. She felt his hand stroke her, moving softly down her belly. His fingers moved along her hip, over the top edge of her panties, and she shivered, aching for him. His hand moved so slowly, so lightly. He stroked down the side of her hip, over her thigh, between her legs. As he continued kissing her, she felt his hand move with agonizing slowness up the inside of her thigh, and held her breath…

But he moved his hand away, cupping her breast. She exhaled, pulling him closer, wanting to feel his weight on her. But he wouldn't be distracted. His hand moved back to her inner thigh, traveling upward frustratingly slowly as she held her breath. Finally he stroked over her panties. He teased her. She gasped as he gently cupped the mound between her thighs.

Kneeling between her legs on the king-size bed, he pulled her silk panties down, down, down. She felt the soft fabric slide like a whisper down her skin. Suddenly naked beneath him, she felt him climb naked on top of her, lowering his head to kiss her. His tongue moved between her lips, his mouth stretched her wide. And she felt him hard and thick at the entrance to the hot center that ached between her thighs. Every inch of their bodies, her soft curves and his hard, muscled form, seemed fused together with need, sweat and fire. Only one part of them had yet to be joined. One part on fire with need. She felt him, huge and hard, nudging against her wet, hot core.

But she was afraid. She braced for him to thrust himself inside her, cleaving her tender flesh, but instead, exhaling, showing visible control, he slowly thrust a single inch inside her. She gasped. She felt so wet, enfolding his enormous shaft. He pushed further, to two inches. He was so thick it ached a little, stretching her, but as he slid inside, it felt good. So good. Just like the first time...

Then she remembered. With a sudden cry, she lifted up on her elbows and breathed, "Condom?"

His dark eyes narrowed, and then he scowled. "I forgot..." He started to reach toward his nightstand. Then he looked down at her with a sensual, slow-rising smile. "I do not need a condom, *querida*. Ever again."

"You—don't?"

"You are my wife." He pulled back his hand, and his expression turned wicked as he looked at her with heavily lidded eyes. "I want to get you pregnant. Now."

"Now?" she said, her eyes wide. It was too soon. She hadn't even had a period yet, since the birth of her baby three months ago. She shook her head. "I'm not ready..."

"We have eight bedrooms," he insisted. "I want to fill them. I want the noise and joy of many children. And I want you as their mother." As he held her wrists, holding her down to the bed, his dark eyes seared hers. "Let me fill you with my baby, *querida*."

Callie stared up at him, feeling pinned to the bed. Was she ready to make that lifelong commitment to Eduardo that he wanted? Ready to be bound to him even further? Even deeper?

He pushed himself back into her, and she closed her eyes, gasping with pleasure. He felt so good inside her. Farther and deeper sounded like all she'd ever wanted. She tried to think about the decision that had to be made but her rational mind fell away as he gripped her hips tight. His huge shaft slowly filled her, inch by inch, sliding through her tight, wet passage.

She gripped his shoulders, her fingernails digging into his skin as she arched her back, her head tilted back. Her whole body was taut and aching with need for more, just a little more. She wanted him to fill her all the way, to ram himself deeply inside her. Her breasts swayed as he penetrated her. Her nipples were taut as he lowered his head to lick one rosy peak. With his rough mouth on her, his hips took decisive action. He thrust deeply inside her, all the way to the hilt, and she nearly screamed with pleasure.

But even then, reality intruded. She'd made this mistake once. Not again. Never again. Her fingers gripped into his shoulders, and she opened her eyes, pushing him back.

"Condom," she panted.

For a long moment, he stared at her. Then his eyes narrowed. Rolling off her, he grabbed a condom from the nightstand and sheathed himself in a quick movement, rolling it down over his thick shaft in the manner of a man who'd done it many, many times. Then he climbed back on top of her. Anger seemed to seep from his body, and Callie licked her lips, wanting to repair the mood between them.

"Thank—"

He put his finger roughly on her lips. "Don't," he ground out.

Gripping her hips with his hands, he thrust himself inside her, all the way to the hilt. She gasped, forgetting their argument, forgetting everything as he rode her, hard and deep. A shudder built inside her, a tremble like an earthquake as he filled her, like an underground river bursting from the cracks of a dam. She felt tension ratchet higher and higher inside her, shaking her. Her head fell back as she held her breath, climbing higher and higher still. She closed her eyes as her lips parted in a soundless cry.

Then it was no longer silent, and she screamed, clutching his shoulders as she exploded.

A low, answering cry came from his lips. His hard, handsome face was pale, as if he'd held himself back by only the slenderest thread. But as she shook and tightened around him in ecstasy, he surrendered. He thrust inside her one last time, impaling her so hard and deep she felt split in two, and he filled her with a hoarse shout, his eyes closed, his face euphoric. Almost reverent.

Collapsing over her sweaty, exhausted body, he held her against his chest. "You will belong to me," he whispered. "You'll soon surrender."

Turning toward him, Callie pressed her cheek against his bare chest. Her own heartbeat roared in her ears. As she drowsed in his powerful arms, exhausted and protected by the warmth and strength of his naked body, she knew it was already true. It had always been true.

Her heart had surrendered long ago.

CHAPTER SEVEN

CALLIE woke up with a start. What time was it? Was that her baby crying?

She rose blearily from bed before she was even quite awake. The moonlight had moved across her bedroom, so she must have slept. With a gasp, she remembered how her husband had just made love to her. She glanced back at the bed with her heart in her throat and a smile on her lips.

The bed was empty. Eduardo was gone.

She glanced at the clock over the mantel on the bedroom's fireplace. Three in the morning. Where could he be? Why would he leave her in the middle of the night, after he'd so thoroughly reclaimed his bed?

Her cheeks grew hot at the memory of last night. He'd claimed her in a way she'd never forget.

Then her baby wailed again from the nursery, louder this time. She hurried through the adjacent door, turning on a little lamp shaped like a giraffe that gave a soft, golden light. She picked up her baby. "It's all right," she soothed. "Mommy's here. I'm here." Cradling her chubby three-month-old baby in her arms, Callie carried her to the gliding chair near the window. As she nursed her child, the baby's complaints faded. Looking down at her, Callie was lost in wonder at her baby's beauty, at the long black eyelashes she'd gotten from Eduardo brushing against her plump cheeks. One of her baby's tiny hands gripped her finger.

We have eight bedrooms. I want to fill them.

What would it be like, Callie thought, to have a whole houseful of babies like this? To have a large family? An adoring husband?

Slowly her eyes looked around the cheerful nursery. It was warm and luxurious, but she would have liked to create her baby's nursery herself, even with just a bucket of paint, a sewing machine and her own two hands—not paying someone else to do it, but doing it herself as a labor of love. Next time, she promised herself. Then stopped.

Next time.

Could she really stay married to Eduardo, knowing he would never love her? He knew how to make love…oh, yes. She shivered, closing her eyes as she remembered how he'd caressed her last night. Remembered the feel of his body against hers. The husky sound of his voice as he'd said, *You belong to me.*

He knew how to make love.

But she'd never seen him truly care for anyone. Except their baby.

Was their lust, and mutual care for their child, enough to sustain a marriage when their values were so different?

After her baby nursed back to sleep, Callie left her on her back in the oval-shaped crib, careful not to wake her. She'd likely sleep another four hours now, or maybe more. Every night, she slept a little longer. Her baby had become an excellent sleeper.

And maybe she would be now, too. Closing the nursery door softly behind her, Callie smiled. The last few hours, after falling asleep in Eduardo's arms, had been the best sleep she'd had all year.

He wanted her to be his wife forever. He wanted them

to be a family. And she'd loved him for years. Even when she'd hated him, it had been the hurt of a woman who'd been rejected from the person she loved most.

Maybe it could work. Maybe it could be enough.

Or maybe, somehow, he would grow to love her, as she loved him. She closed her eyes, hugging herself at the thought. If there was even the slightest chance of him loving her someday, she would have married him at once. Remembering, she bleakly opened her eyes. No wonder Eduardo had called her *naive* and *ridiculously sentimental.*

Where was he, anyway? She looked around her dark, empty bedroom. Where could he be at this time of the night?

Maybe he'd gone to the kitchen for a snack.

Pulling on a soft blue chenille robe, she went downstairs, but the kitchen was dark and empty. Walking past the wall of windows with its magnificent view of the city, she went down the hall to his home office, then to the theater room, then even past Mrs. McAuliffe's suite. She could hear the older woman's soft snoring muffled through the door. Puzzled, Callie finally went back upstairs.

Glancing in the empty guest rooms, she had just decided to phone their bodyguard in his separate apartment downstairs when she heard Eduardo's voice in the guest room.

"Nothing has changed." His voice was the smooth, arrogant tone she remembered. "Nothing."

With an intake of breath, she pulled back from the doorway, leaning against the wall of the dark hallway with one hand over her mouth and the other over her heart.

"Don't call here again," he growled, and hung up.

A little squeak escaped her lips. Who was Eduardo talking to? An old lover? Was that why he'd snuck out of bed to talk to someone in private, so his wife couldn't hear? Even as Callie tried to tell herself that she was overreacting, that he could be talking to anyone, her heart was gripped with fear.

There has been no other woman since the night you were in my bed. Do you understand what I am telling you? No other woman.

She exhaled as the vise grip on her heart loosened. Eduardo was not a liar. If anything, he was cruelly honest. As his secretary, she'd seen him callously dispose of one lover after another, plainly telling them to their faces that he was bored with them, or that he had absolutely no intention of being faithful. He was not a liar.

But then, he'd never had to lie. He'd never been married before.

"What are you doing awake?"

With an intake of breath, she saw him in the doorway, looking down at her with dark eyes. "Um…" Her fingers fidgeted with the belt of her blue chenille robe. "I got up to feed Marisol and you were gone."

"I didn't want to wake you." His handsome face was impassive. "I couldn't sleep."

"Oh. I'm sorry." She bit her lip, feeling guilty that she'd slept so well. "Is something wrong? Was I snoring, or…"

He gave a low laugh then shook his head soberly. "I just don't sleep well with other people in my bed. I have never managed it."

She frowned. "Never?"

"Have you ever heard of me letting a woman sleep over?"

Callie stared at him, remembering when he'd been her boss, the most heartless playboy in the city. "N-no," she said hesitantly. She gave him an awkward smile. "You were kind of famous for your one-*hour* stands, actually."

He leaned against the door frame, looking down at the floor. "It's hard to let down my guard."

"Even with me?"

He looked up. "Especially with you," he whispered.

The low lights of the hallway caused hard shadows across the angles and planes of Eduardo's face. His jawline was dark with stubble, giving him a piratical air. He looked like a pirate all over, in fact. A sexy, dangerous, hard-bodied pirate. Without thinking, she put a hand on his warm, hard, bare chest above drawstring cotton pajama pants slung low on his slender hips.

"Is there anything I could do to help you sleep?" Realizing how blatant that sounded, she blushed. "I mean, could I get you some warm milk or something?"

"No," he said abruptly then amended, "but thanks."

She looked at him. "Why didn't you kick me out?" she whispered. "Last Christmas, the night I stayed at your house?"

His eyes met hers. "You weren't just some starlet I picked up at a gala. You were important to me. I wanted you to stay."

"You did?" she breathed. "Why?"

"Don't you know?" Pulling her into his arms, he lifted her chin to meet his gaze. Then he smiled…the charming, megawatt smile that always twisted her heart in a million pieces. "I need you, Callie."

Eduardo looked at his wife in the shadows of the hallway. Her pale cheeks were rosy, her emerald eyes bright, and her light brown hair, long and wavy, fell over the shoulders of her blue robe. She was so sexy, so soft and desirable. He'd just had her, and already he wanted her again. He wanted her even more.

Callie's eyes filled up with tears.

"You need me? I thought…I thought you only wanted me here because of the baby."

He moved toward her, gently brushing her hair off her shoulders. "That's not the only reason."

Trembling, she looked up at him. Words seemed to tremble on her lips, but at the last moment, she turned away. Staring down the dark, quiet hall, she wrapped her arms around her body. The sleeves of the blue chenille robe hung long over her wrists, making her look like a kid playing dress-up.

"I want to stay with you," she said softly. "And be your wife."

Eduardo's heart rose with fierce triumph. "*Querida*—"

She held up her hand. Her green eyes were luminous. "But I will no longer neglect and ignore my friends and family just to coddle your insecurity."

Her harsh words were like a slap across the jaw. His eyes widened then narrowed. "*Coddle* my *insecurity*." His voice was low and dangerous. "You mean how I've forbidden you to talk to Brandon McLinn."

"Yes."

Jaw tight, he took a step toward her. "You should just let him go."

"No." Her eyes glittered defiantly. "He's my friend."

"Friend!" he snarled. He shook his head. "He told me you'd been engaged since high school. He said even if you'd fallen into bed with me, I meant nothing to you and that you'd soon be done with me—"

Eduardo stopped, his jaw tight, his heart pounding. He hadn't meant to say so much. Brow furrowed, Callie came closer, and the soft light from the guest room illuminated her pale, beautiful face. She gave an awkward laugh.

"Want to hear a funny story? At senior prom, we made this silly pact that if we weren't married by the time we were thirty, we would marry each other."

"You're only twenty-five."

"Yes, I know. I'm starting to wonder if perhaps Brandon was—" she licked her lips uncomfortably "—well, maybe threatened by you."

Suddenly it all made sense.

Eduardo sucked in his breath. "You weren't in love with him, were you? He was trying to get rid of me, and it worked." He clawed back his hair with his hand. "Once I was out of the way, he used your pregnancy as an excuse to move in for the kill."

Drawing back in confusion, Callie shook her head. "He loves me, yes, but like a brother!"

"I was such a fool." Pacing two steps down the hall, he could hardly believe his own stupidity. That night, that beautiful Christmas Eve night when they'd first made love, when he'd taken Callie's virginity, he'd thought their relationship might be different from all the rest. But he'd thrown away that precious connection—based on the insinuations of his rival!

"Brandon McLinn is in love with you," he ground out. "I saw it in his face."

"He must have been trying to protect me."

"You may be blind to his true feelings. I am not." His eyes narrowed. "You will never contact him again. Or your family."

"What?" Callie's mouth fell open. "What does my family have to do with anything?"

Eduardo couldn't explain, or she would find out everything he'd been keeping from her—for her own good. "I am your husband. You will trust me and obey."

"Obey?" Callie glared at him, folding her arms. "What century are you in? You might be my husband, but you are no longer my boss!"

"Am I not?" he said softly. He reached his hand to her cheek, stroking softly down her neck. She closed her eyes, and he felt her shudder beneath his touch. "I am trying to protect our family. I have my reasons. Believe me."

But Callie stiffened, stepping back, out of his reach. "No."

His eyes widened then his brows lowered. "No?"

"I want to be your wife, Eduardo. I do," she whispered. "But I have to see my family. And Brandon."

"I could take you to court. The prenuptial agreement—"

"So do it." She looked at him evenly. "Take me to court."

She was calling his bluff. He had no desire to sue his own wife, the mother of his baby. And now they both knew it. He exhaled, clenching his hands. "I will not allow you to—"

"It's not a question of you *allowing* me. I'm telling you. I need a relationship with my family—including Brandon— and so does Marisol. I'm going home to visit my family. You can divorce me. But you can't stop me."

Checkmate, he thought, almost with despair.

He still couldn't forget—or forgive—the way her parents had treated Callie when she'd called them just two hours after the birth, anxious to tell them about the baby. She'd had every reason to relax and get some rest, but instead she'd tried to share the joyous news with her mother and father. She'd been left sobbing with grief. The memory still made his jaw clench.

Eduardo had always dreamed of having a family of his own. A family that was kind and loving, not cruel or harsh as his own had been.

He wouldn't let anyone make Callie cry like that. Ever.

Staring at her, a thought took hold of his brain. Morally reprehensible—but then, he thought grimly, he was already in so deep he might as well go a little further.

It was for her own good, he repeated to himself. For her own good, and the safety of their little family.

"Have you considered, *querida*," he said in a low voice, "that perhaps they might not want to see you?"

Callie looked at him with stricken eyes. "What?"

It was cold, it was cruel, it was wrong. But he pushed aside his twinges of conscience. He had to be ruthless. "Has McLinn contacted you once in the last three months?" He tilted his head. "Has anyone in your family tried to call you back, even once?"

Her folded arms fell, and she looked uncertain. "No." Swallowing, she blinked fast. "But I can't blame them. I let them down."

"No," he said sharply. "You had a baby. You got married. And when you tried to share that news with them, they ripped you apart."

She took a deep breath. "I know it might seem that way…"

"They were cruel to you." He could still remember the rasp of her father's voice. *You'll never be a decent husband or father, and you know it. If you're even half a man, you'll send her and the baby home to people who are capable of loving them.*

"I'll make them forgive me." Callie's emerald eyes glittered suspiciously. "I have to try."

As she turned away, he grabbed her arm. "Write to them first."

She turned back to face him. "What?"

"If you show up in person, who knows how they'll react? What if they shut the door in your face? Do you really want to risk it?"

Callie looked pale, staring at him.

"Write first," he said smoothly. "It's the best way to gather your thoughts. And give them time to consider theirs."

"Well." She took a deep breath, her expression crestfallen. "Maybe you're right." She looked down at her feet. "I would die if they shut the door in my face. Or if they refused to see Marisol. I can't even imagine it. But then," she said unhappily, "I thought they would call me before now…."

He put his hands around her shoulders. "Write to them."

"You think so?"

"Absolutely."

She bit her lip. "Even Brandon?"

Exhaling, jaw tight, he gave a single nod.

She sighed. "All right."

"All right?"

She looked up. Her green eyes were bright, her cheeks flushed. "Thank you," she said haltingly, "for helping me. I don't know what I'd do without you."

Eduardo had never seen her look so beautiful. Mesmerized, he reached down to stroke her cheek then pulled her into his arms. He felt her soft breasts press against his chest, and breathed in the floral and vanilla scent of her hair. He felt the warm whisper of her breath against his bare chest, and his drawstring pajamas suddenly felt three sizes too tight. "I told you," he said hoarsely. "I don't want your thanks."

"But—"

"Don't." Especially since he had no intention of allowing her letters to reach her family—or McLinn. He put his palm against her cheek, his fingers threading through her hair. "You are my woman, Callie. I would do anything to keep you safe and happy."

Looking up at him, she suddenly blurted out, "Who were you talking to on the phone?"

He stared at her. "What?"

Looking grumpy, she folded her arms. "I wasn't going

to ask," she sighed. "I was going to be totally stoic and silent about it."

"Oh, *querida.*" Smiling, Eduardo stroked her cheek. She was so transparent. He loved that about her. "You wondered if I was talking to some woman?"

"The thought crossed my mind. Every woman wants you.…"

"And I want only one woman in the world." Lifting her chin, he looked straight into her eyes. "I am yours and only yours, my beautiful wife. I will never betray you, Callie."

"You won't?"

"I was just talking to a rival…who lives far away."

"Oh," she said. With a sigh of relief, she hugged him, pressing her face against his bare chest.

Stroking her back through the soft chenille robe, Eduardo exhaled at how close it had been. She must have heard the end of his phone call. If she'd heard the whole conversation, she wouldn't have been worried about some imaginary woman. No, it would have been far more dire.

"Try to contact my wife again," Eduardo had growled, "and you'll regret it."

"You can't keep me from her. We both know you're not good enough. You'll never make her happy." McLinn's voice had been angry, and with an edge of desperation that had grown over the months Eduardo had blocked the man's letters and phone calls. Yesterday, there had even been an attempted delivery of a cell phone in a padded envelope. His bodyguard had opened the package while Callie was upstairs getting ready for the Winter Ball.

An hour ago, Eduardo's anger had finally boiled over. Rising from their bed as Callie slept, he'd used the number from his investigator, and called McLinn's cell phone in the middle of the night.

The young farmer had actually threatened him, saying he was going to call the police and claim Callie was being held against her will. Against her will!

Eduardo narrowed his eyes. The police he could deal with. But McLinn had threatened to return to New York. He could not guard Callie at every moment in the city, keeping her from any unexpected meeting. Nor could he risk letting her talk to McLinn. He could only imagine what the man would tell her.

He needed a third option.

From the day they'd wed, he'd assigned the same investigator who got dirt on business competitors to keep track of his wife and all her family. Eduardo had burned the angry letters sent by her father, the pleading tearstained cards from her mother. He'd tossed her sister's bouquet of sappy flowers shaped like a pink baby carriage in the trash.

At first he'd done it because he didn't trust Callie. Then he told himself he was just trying to protect her. Sure, her father was trying to be nicer now, but even Eduardo's own parents had had their good days. He wouldn't allow them access to Callie until he knew for sure they wouldn't hurt her again.

But deep in his heart, he knew that wasn't the only reason.

You weren't even man enough to come and ask me for her hand. The memory of her father's cold words still rankled in his mind. *You might own half our town, but I know the kind of man you really are. You'll never be a decent husband or father, and you know it.*

To Walter, as to many others, Eduardo was just a selfish, demanding tyrant, the foreign CEO that his employees obeyed—but despised.

So be it. Eduardo didn't need the man's respect. But he

wouldn't let anyone insult his wife. Or cause them problems that could tear his family apart.

Stroking her back, Eduardo took a deep breath. He was starting to trust Callie again. But he didn't trust the world. Whenever he let himself care for someone, they disappeared from his life. He wouldn't let that happen. Not this time.

"Eduardo?"

Callie was looking up at him in the shadowy hallway, her brow furrowed. Her robe had fallen open slightly to reveal her plump breasts, and suddenly he knew exactly what he needed. He pulled her closer, stroking the edge of her neckline as he murmured, "You said something about helping me sleep?"

"Er." She suddenly blushed. "I just thought…"

"Yes." Grabbing her hand, he led her back to the master bedroom. Pulling the robe off her unresisting body, he pushed her back against the bed. His wife looked like an angel in the moonlight, he thought, her light brown hair silver twined with gold, her pale skin luminous. Her breasts were huge, their full rosy tips bright and vivid against her white skin.

Eduardo kissed her hard and deep. He felt her respond, kissing him back with equal fire, and wanted her as if he hadn't already been satiated that night. He wanted her even more than he did yesterday, and all the year before that. Her small hands roamed his body, stroking his naked chest, caressing his shoulders, his back. He exhaled when she ran her fingers lightly over his backside then groaned aloud as she ran her hand questingly over the hard shaft beneath his drawstring pajama pants. Her face was rapt as she stroked his hard length through the fabric. He grabbed her wrist.

"I do not know—how long I can last," he groaned.

She gave him a smile full of infinite feminine mystery. "So don't."

"*Querida*—"

She unlaced his pants and pulled them down his hips, to his thighs. His hard shaft sprung free from the fabric, and she looked down at him with awe. Reaching out, she took him fully in her hands.

"Callie," he breathed. Her touch felt too good, causing him to jerk involuntarily beneath her stroke. His heart was pounding. He wanted to bury himself deep inside her, impale her, fill her to the hilt now—now—*now*! "What are you—?"

Her eyes were dark and full of need as she pulled him over her onto the bed. "Take me," she whispered.

A low growl rose in his throat as he looked down at her, spread across the bed for his pleasure. He didn't even take the time to pull off his pajama pants. He couldn't. Leaving them across his thighs, he positioned himself and thrust inside her, filling her.

She gasped, gripping his shoulders. Her face filled with anguished ecstasy, and for a moment he thought he'd gone too far, too deep. He started to withdraw.

"No." Gripping her fingers into his flesh, she started to move beneath him. "More."

He pushed inside her again, and she moaned. He rode her, harder and faster, until the bed frame rocked loudly against the wall.

"Stop!" she whispered, looking up at him. "Don't wake the baby!"

He exhaled in a surprised laugh then, leaning forward, kissed her forehead tenderly. Gripping her hips, he slowly thrust inside her in a controlled movement. Somehow the silence just deepened the pleasure. Made it forbidden. He rode her wet and hard until she gripped his upper arms and he heard her soundless scream of pleasure. With a rush of ecstasy, he slammed into her one last time with a shuddering, silent gasp as his whole world shimmered and exploded.

He fell on top of her. It might have been minutes, or an hour, later before he was aware he might be crushing her beneath the weight of his body. He didn't know how much time had passed, which was strange. For one precious moment, it had almost felt like sleep....

He started to move away from her, but she grabbed his arm. "Stay with me."

He hesitated. He knew he wouldn't be able to sleep beside her. But in this moment, he could deny her nothing. Without a word, he rolled back and pulled her to his naked chest, spooning her smaller body with his larger one.

She turned around in his arms. "I love you."

Shocked, he stared down at her in the dark bedroom. Her beautiful, round, upturned face was glowing, tears sparkling down her cheeks in the moonlight.

"I love you, Eduardo." Closing her eyes, she pressed her cheek against his bare chest. "I never stopped loving you, and I never will."

A tremble went through his body as he stroked her hair. Hearing those words on his wife's lips—the words he'd detested and avoided hearing from any other woman—was a sudden, precious gift. Sweet beyond measure.

Poison in his heart.

Now he had even more to lose. Even more to protect. His arms tightened around her. Would she still love him if she found out what he'd done? After Brandon McLinn explained it to her in the most destructive way possible?

He said with forced cheerfulness, "What do you think about spending Christmas in the south of Spain?"

Pressing her face against his chest, she gave a contented sigh. "Spain?"

He stroked her back, keeping his voice casual. "I have a villa on the coast, not too far from my old village." *And five thousand miles from Brandon McLinn.* "What do you say?"

She smiled up at him sleepily. "I'll go anywhere with you."

Eduardo gloried in his wife's generous spirit and trusting heart. Callie knew his flaws better than anyone. And yet somehow she'd chosen to love him.

It was the most precious gift he'd ever received. And the one he least deserved.

Within minutes, she fell asleep in his arms. Eduardo stared out the windows at the dark city and the vast blackness of the Hudson River. It was cold December, when night lasted forever and spring was a distant promise. She loved him. And it was like hot summer to a half-frozen man.

He would never let her go. Ever. Even if it cost his very soul.

In the darkness, his eyes hardened.

He wouldn't lose her. Not now. Not ever.

CHAPTER EIGHT

SITTING by their pool overlooking the Mediterranean, Callie was trying—again—to convince her body to tan in the warm Spanish sun. She glanced back toward their luxurious, enormous villa, where her baby was taking her afternoon nap. Callie loved it here. All right, she was still shockingly pale, but she'd never been so happy.

Or so sad.

In the four months since they'd left New York, her handsome husband had taken their family all over the world via private jet, to all the glamorous places she'd once dreamed of as a girl. They'd spent Christmas here at the villa, decorating their enormous Christmas tree with oranges. On Christmas Eve, they'd gone to a candlelight service, then after putting the baby to bed she and Eduardo had a midnight supper by candlelight. It had been a special, sacred night between them, the one-year anniversary of the first time they'd made love.

When she woke the next morning, Eduardo was gone, as always. Getting Marisol from her crib, she'd gone downstairs to discover an obscene number of gifts beneath their Christmas tree, and beside it, a debonair Santa with twinkling black eyes, in a red suit far too large for his sleek physique and a fake white beard over his chiseled jawline. Marisol had laughed in wonder and delight, and so had

Callie. Santa had presented their baby with so many expensive toys and clothes that it could have satisfied a child army. Marisol had responded by playing with the tissue paper and then trying to chew on her own shoe.

Callie had giggled. "See what happens when you spend too much money on a baby, Santa?"

Santa turned to her. "And I have something for you, Mrs. Claus, er, Cruz."

Reaching into his big black bag, he'd pulled out a key chain that had her initials, "CC", created in what looked to be diamonds and gold. She'd taken the key chain with an incredulous laugh.

"It's beautiful...but are you crazy? People lose key chains. I'll be scared to use this."

Santa smirked. "The key chain isn't the gift. Look again."

Frowning, she looked down at the ridiculously expensive gold-and-diamond key chain and saw the key. Her mouth went dry as she looked up. "What's this?"

He gave her a sudden wicked grin. "Go outside."

Still in her red-and-green flannel pajamas, she'd lifted their baby on her hip, and gone out into the courtyard of the villa, with Santa close behind. Even on Christmas Day, the Spanish sun was warm, and the air smelled of orange groves and the ocean. She'd stopped abruptly in the dusty courtyard.

There, with a big red bow on the hood, she saw a brand-new Rolls-Royce.

"The silver reminded me of you," he murmured softly behind her. "It's the color of the dress you wore to the Winter Ball a few weeks ago. You sparkled like a diamond. You shone like a star."

Turning to face him without a word, Callie pulled down

his white beard. Eduardo's handsome face was revealed, his dark eyes glowing with admiration.

"And every day, Mrs. Cruz," he said, stroking her cheek, "you're more beautiful still."

With an intake of breath, she threw one arm around his neck and, standing on tiptoe, gave Santa the kiss of his life. It wasn't until Marisol began to squirm and complain that Callie recalled that she was squashing their baby, and that she probably shouldn't let her baby see her kissing Santa Claus anyway.

Callie drew back with tears in her eyes.

"Thank you," she whispered, then shook her head with a laugh. "But I'm afraid you're going to be very disappointed with my gift to you."

"What is it?"

"Soap-on-a-rope and a really ugly tie," she teased.

"Oh, yeah? I've been needing those."

She smiled at him. In reality it was a homemade coffee mug she and Marisol had made together, etched with her baby's tiny handprints, which she knew he'd love.

He sobered. "You give me a gift every day, Callie," he said softly. "By being my wife."

She'd looked at him, her heart in her throat. Then her smile faltered. "I just wish I'd heard from my family today."

Eduardo's eyes darkened, and he gave her a tight smile that didn't meet his eyes. "Do not worry, *querida*. I am sure you will hear from them soon."

But she hadn't, not in all the months since then. She'd sent her parents and her sister a letter every week, filled with photographs of Marisol and of their life in Europe. She'd told them how the baby was growing. She'd told them about Marisol's first tooth, the first time she'd turned over in her crib, the first time she'd sat up by herself. She'd described everything that had happened over the seven months of her baby's life. Callie had even poured out her feelings about Eduardo, her former boss, whom she'd once tried to hate but now loved. She wanted to undo the damage she'd once done, and let them see Eduardo as he really was: a good man.

In response to all her carefully written letters, she'd gotten only cold silence.

She tried not to let it bother her. When Eduardo was home, he gave her and the baby his full attention. He'd needed to take business trips again, to the Arctic and Colombia and elsewhere. But whenever he traveled to a destination he thought his family might enjoy, he brought Callie and Marisol along, traveling on the private jet with a full staff and Mrs. McAuliffe in tow. It was amazing.

They'd spent Valentine's Day in Paris, in a royal suite at a five-star hotel with a view of the *Tour Eiffel*. After the baby was asleep, Eduardo had surprised Callie with a romantic, private dinner for two in their suite. She shivered, remembering champagne, chocolate-dipped strawberries and hot kisses that had lasted for hours.

Most recently, they'd gone to Italy. In Venice, he'd rented a palace overlooking the Grand Canal and they'd shared a romantic gondola ride; in Rome, Marisol had had her first taste of lemon gelato, which she'd savored by letting it dribble down her chin.

Such adventures they'd shared as a family. Growing up on her parents' rural farm, the farthest Callie had ever traveled as a child was to the county fair. She'd never have imagined she'd someday have a life like this. International. Glamorous.

Now, the afternoon sun lowered behind the swaying palm trees as Callie sat beside the gorgeous infinity pool back at their villa. She turned her face toward the blue sky.

Taking a drink of cold, lemon-flavored water, she closed her eyes, stretching out on the lounge chair, relishing the warm Spanish sun on her cheeks.

Seven months of marriage and she still wasn't pregnant. But Eduardo never seemed to tire of trying. He wanted her pregnant. Each night, after they made love, he held her till she slept before he slipped away to the nearest guest room to sleep alone. She hated waking up alone. But that was a tiny thing, nothing really, compared to the multitude of joys in her life, with her baby and husband she loved.

But she still missed the family she'd left behind in North Dakota. It was a heartache that never quite went away.

Her letters hadn't worked, in spite of her best efforts. Her eyes flew open and she stared up at the blue sky. Maybe it was time to do something drastic.

"Callie."

She heard her husband's voice across the pool. Lifting her head, she smiled as she watched him walk toward her, wearing only swimming trunks that showed off his tanned, magnificent body. She could not look away from his hard-muscled torso, powerful arms and strong thighs. The sensual way he moved seduced her—without him even trying!

"I like seeing you by the pool," he said appreciatively. Lifting a dark eyebrow, he looked over her pale body in her tiny bikini. "You look hot, in all those clothes."

She giggled. "You always say that. You told me I looked hot when it was pouring rain in London in January. I was shivering like a drowned rat and you started taking off my clothes!"

"I'm always available to help take off your clothes." Taking her hand in his own, he said innocently, "Care for a nice refreshing swim?"

Eduardo had a look in his dark eyes that made her suspect their "nice refreshing swim" would soon lead to rampant nakedness for them both. The heat in his gaze left her breathless. Her husband didn't seem to see any flaws in her post-pregnancy figure. He called her *beautiful, gorgeous,* and *irresistible*, and once she was naked in his arms, he told her so with his body.

"All right." Smiling, Callie let him pull her to her feet and lead her into the pool. The bobbing water felt cool against her bikini and sun-warmed skin. Once in the deep end of the pool, he pulled her into his arms and kissed her.

His lips felt hot and hard against hers. She clung to him as he kissed her, relishing the feel of his hard, muscled body towering over her petite frame. She loved him so much. And though he hadn't spoken those three words back to her, she was convinced it was just a matter of time…

He pulled back with a shiver. "Oh, *querida*," he said hoarsely. "I'm going to miss you."

"Miss me?" She blinked. "Where are you going?"

As they held each other in the pool, the water bobbing against her breasts, he stroked her cheek with a scowl. "Marrakech. To complete a business deal."

"Morocco? For how long?"

"Hard to say. The man is unpredictable. The negotiations might last a day—or a week."

"A week? A full week at the villa without you? I can't face it."

"I'll miss you, too."

She took a deep breath. "But it might be the perfect time for me to visit my parents. I'll just take the other jet while you're gone…"

He frowned. "What?"

She met his eyes. "I've been writing my family every week for four months. It's not working. I need to go see them."

Eduardo stared at her. Was it just her imagination, or did some of the color disappear behind his tan? "Absolutely not."

"Why?" She tilted her head, folding her arms. She'd expected a fight and was ready for it. "You won't exactly miss us. You'll be in Morocco."

"Maybe I'd like you and Marisol to come with me. Marrakech is beautiful in April."

"That wasn't your plan a minute ago."

"Plans change."

As the cool water of the pool bobbed around them, they glared at each other. Above them, the wind blew through the palm trees, and she could hear the roar of the distant ocean as seabirds cried out mournfully across the cloudless blue sky.

And Callie broke. "I miss them, Eduardo." She unfolded her arms, blinking back tears. "I don't know what else to do. I miss them."

He set his jaw. "I thought you were happy here—"

"I am. But I *miss* them. Every hour. Every day. It's like a hole in my heart." She put her hand over his chest. "Right here." Tears streamed down her cheeks as she looked up at him. "I can't stand the silence. I feel lost without them."

Eduardo stared at her for a long moment. Then, closing his eyes, he exhaled.

"All right," he said in a low voice.

"All right?"

He looked down at her. "Not McLinn. But your parents and your sister—yes."

"I can go see them in North Dakota?" she breathed, hardly able to believe it.

"But I don't want you and Marisol so far away from me. And I need to be in Marrakech tomorrow..."

Her heart, which had been rising, suddenly pinched. She said dully, "So I should put off my visit."

"No." Taking her in his arms, he gently lifted her chin. "I will charter a jet to collect your family. If they agree, they will meet us in Marrakech tomorrow. How about that?"

She stared at him, shocked.

"You will see them. And they will get a chance to meet me." His jaw clenched as he looked away. "Not just as the CEO who owns the oilfields outside your town, but as your husband. As Marisol's father." He looked back at her, his darkly handsome face suddenly uncertain. "Is… is that satisfactory?"

"Satisfactory!" she cried. She threw her arms around him in the pool and kissed him, over and over, kissed his cheeks, his forehead, his chin. "Oh, Eduardo, I love you so much. Thank you, my darling, thank you!"

He straightened in the pool. His hard-muscled body dazzled her. Droplets of water cascaded down his tanned skin, sparkling in the sun as he lifted her up, wrapping her legs around his waist.

"This time," he whispered, "I'll let you thank me."

And he kissed her, long and hard, beneath the waving palm trees and the hot Spanish sun.

Many hours later, Eduardo looked down at his naked wife, sleeping in his arms in the darkness of the bedroom. It was past midnight. And he wanted to sleep with her.

Not just make love to her. Making love was easy. Callie was damn beautiful. A man would have to be dead not to want her constantly. Especially when she was happy, as she'd been today.

She'd been so thrilled to speak with her parents on the phone that afternoon. She hadn't noticed how shocked her parents were to hear from her, and learn she was in Spain. But after tears on both sides, the Woodvilles had agreed to take his chartered jet and join them in Morocco, after a quick stop at the American consulate to get their very first passports.

Later that evening, as Eduardo discussed necessary travel arrangements with his assistant, Callie had bounced off the walls with excitement and joy. After dinner, they'd played with the baby, given Marisol a bath and put her to bed, and then Callie had grabbed his hand and pulled him to bed, too. Even after making love for hours, for the second time that day, it had still taken unusually long for Callie to fall asleep in his arms: a full ten minutes.

That was hours ago. Eduardo looked bleakly across the luxurious master bedroom of the villa. God knew he'd tried to make himself sleep. But it was always the same. After they made love, he would hold her, his body relaxed, his soul in perfect, blissful peace. He would cherish her in his arms, so soft and willing and warm. But the instant he closed his eyes, sleep disappeared. He tried to relax, but his muscles became tight until beads of sweat broke out on his forehead.

He'd never slept with any of the women he bedded. But he'd never wanted to. He'd thought it would be different with Callie. But even with her, he still couldn't let down his guard completely. Eduardo exhaled, knowing he wasn't going to be able to sleep tonight, either. He should get up and go to the guest room to sleep, like usual.

Yet he wanted to sleep with his wife.

He wanted to deserve her.

Since the day they'd wed, Eduardo had done everything he could to keep his family safe and happy. He'd supported Callie in every way.

Except one. None of her letters to her family had ever

left the house. And she'd never gotten any of their mail, forwarded from New York. When Sami Woodville had tried to phone his office, he'd instructed his secretary to block her calls. When she'd called his cell phone, he'd changed his number.

A cold chill went through his body. Would Callie ever forgive him when she discovered what he'd done? Would she understand that he'd done it for one reason: to protect their family?

He'd been ruthless for a reason. But when Callie had wept with grief in the pool today, something had snapped inside him, and he couldn't do it anymore—even though he knew all hell would break loose when she spoke with her parents and put two and two together. It was remotely possible for the mail service to misplace a letter, but not scores of them. Callie would soon figure out who'd had means and motive to suppress them.

Eduardo stared bleakly at the bedroom ceiling.

He should tell her himself what he'd done, rather than letting her figure it out. Rather than—say—letting Brandon McLinn be the one to tell her. His jaw tightened. He was sick of feeling the ghost of McLinn always at his back. Tired of waiting for the moment when Callie would finally be disgusted by Eduardo's flawed soul and leave. Tired of feeling Brandon McLinn always waiting in the shadows, ready to take Callie away the instant he made a mistake.

Was this that final mistake?

His arms tightened around Callie.

Her parents and sister were already somewhere over the Atlantic, but his investigator was having trouble tracking down Brandon McLinn. He believed the young farmer might be on his way, even now, to southern Spain, since he'd discovered their villa's location from Callie's family.

Eduardo allowed himself a grim smile. By the time he arrived here, Callie would be in Morocco.

The smile faded as he looked at Callie's slumbering, trusting face. He should pull his private investigator off Brandon McLinn, along with Walter, Jane and Sami Woodville. He should stop going through his wife's mail or screening her calls at the villa. He should just take a deep breath, and trust her. Trust everyone.

But he couldn't. It would mean flying blind. If Eduardo didn't know the future, how could he prevent catastrophe? How could he keep his family safe? How could he make sure she would never leave, never break his heart; never break Marisol's?

Listening to her quiet, even breathing, he squeezed his eyes shut. His whole body was tense, and sleep danced away from him, mocking him.

Wearily sitting up, Eduardo watched the gray light of dawn through the windows, and heard the faint call of morning birds above the roar of the ocean. He put his head in his hands. He wanted to deserve her. He wanted to trust her.

He wanted to love her.

"Eduardo?"

He felt a gentle hand on his back. He turned, and saw Callie looking up at him with luminous eyes. "What is it?"

He looked down at her. She was naked, and beautiful, and unafraid. He said in a low voice, "I had a dream that you left me."

Her eyes went wide. She sat up, shaking her head. "No." Reaching for him, she pulled him back into the soft comfort of her arms. "That will never happen. Never."

Reaching out, he twined his fingers in her hair. "My parents loved each other once," he said. "They wanted a child. They built a home. Then they grew apart, twisted by secrets and lies. My mother met a new man, and my father was destroyed by it. Everything ended."

Callie took both his hands in her own. "That won't happen to us."

Blinking fast, he looked out at the gray dawn. "I had a dream."

Callie stared at him, suddenly frowning.

"But you don't sleep," she said slowly. "You don't dream."

Eduardo turned to her. She was so beautiful, his wife. So gentle and kind. She believed the best of everyone, even when they didn't deserve it. He took a deep, shuddering breath.

"I do now," he whispered.

CHAPTER NINE

CALLIE'S hands and feet bounced rhythmically against the interior of their four-wheel drive as they drove from the Marrakech airport. Eduardo, who was driving beside her, reached out and stilled her knee with his hand.

"Sorry." She looked up at him with an apologetic smile. "I'm excited."

"Yes." He smiled back at her, his dark eyes warm. "I know." Then a troubled shadow crossed his expression, and he turned away to focus on the road, gripping the wheel.

Business negotiations usually didn't faze Eduardo. Callie wondered why he seemed so tense. He generally relished a good fight. Shrugging it off, she cooed at their baby in her car seat behind them. Through the back window she saw the other vehicle following with their staff and bodyguards as they drove past the twelfth-century ramparts of the medina to the vast sprawling palm desert beyond. The sky was blue above the distant, snowcapped Atlas Mountains.

She turned back to her dark, impossibly handsome husband beside her. He was wearing a business suit, but his dark coloring and black hair made him look like a sheikh. In her own long purple caftan, with the window rolled down and the warm Moroccan wind blowing through her hair, she felt like a cosseted Arabian princess at his side.

It was officially the happiest day of her life. After today, she'd have no reason to ever be sad again.

"Thank you," she said for the millionth time.

Eduardo gave her a sideways glance. "Stop."

"You don't know what this means to me—"

"I mean it." His jaw was tight as he turned off the main road to a guardhouse. Pulling up to a heavily scrolled metal gate, Eduardo spoke in French to a security guard, who with a very deep bow, swung open the gate. Eduardo drove up a long sweeping driveway with the other car behind them.

Callie looked up through the front windshield, her eyes wide when she saw the enormous Moroccan *riad*, two stories tall and surrounded by gardens. Willowy palm trees graced the edges of large swimming pool that sparkled a brilliant blue in the sun. The grand house itself was the combination of traditional Moroccan architecture and old French glamour. Craning her head, Callie looked up with awe at the home's soaring curves and the exquisitely detailed scrollwork. "What is this place?"

"In the 1920s it was a hotel. Now it belongs to Kasimir Xendzov, who loaned it for our visit."

"He's not staying here?"

"No."

She turned to Eduardo in shock. "Why would he leave a place like this?"

He shook his head. "He is in the city as little as possible. He prefers to live like a nomad in the desert." His lips curved. "Like those sheikhs, in the romance novels you love."

"But he's Russian?"

"The local people call him the Tsar of the Desert."

"Oh." The romantic phrase made her shiver. "What's he like?"

"Kasimir? As cold and heartless as his brother. You re-member Vladimir Xendzov?"

She tilted her head. "Prince Vladimir? The man who stole the Yukon deal from us?"

"He's not really a prince, no matter what he says. But yes. They're brothers. They've spent the last ten years try-ing to destroy each other."

Callie stared at him, aghast. "That's awful!"

Eduardo smiled with satisfaction. "A fact that will help me get what I want."

"Prince Vladimir was vicious," she said, troubled. "Corrupt. Definitely unsafe."

"And not a prince."

She pressed her lips together. "Is it smart to make a deal with his brother?"

"Don't worry. We are safe here. Kasimir is our host. His honor is at stake." Pulling the car up to the front of the house, he turned off the engine. Getting out, he handed the keys to a waiting servant. Callie stepped out behind him with her seven-month-old baby in her arms, and heard the soft water of a fountain. She looked at the huge house be-neath the hard blue sky of the desert, and saw a shadow move in the window.

"Are they here?" she whispered.

Eduardo gave her a single, silent nod, and an involun-tary shiver went through her. She walked towards the *riad*, her baby against her hip, her husband and bodyguards fol-lowing behind them.

The house seemed Moorish in design, with a flat roof and intricate tile work. They walked through the soar-ing arches to the door. Inside, the walls were decorated with floral and geometric motifs, intertwined flowers and vines in green, red and gold-leaf paint all the way to the ceiling. Past the foyer was a cloister, an outdoor walkway built around a lush courtyard garden. Callie took a deep breath of the fresh air, listening to the sound of a burbling fountain mingling with birdsong.

Then she heard a woman's scream.

Whirling around, Carrie instinctively held up her arm, protecting her baby from the unseen danger.

But there was no danger, just her sister, racing at her full blast!

"Sami," Callie cried then she looked behind her and saw the smiling eyes of her parents. "Mom! Dad!"

"Callie." Her mother was openly weeping as she pulled her into her arms. "And is this your baby? My grandchild?"

"Yes, it's Marisol," Callie choked out. Her mother sobbed, wrapping Marisol and Callie into a hug with Sami. Her father wrapped his large form around the whole family and she saw to her shock that he, too, was weeping—something she'd never seen in her whole life.

"I missed you all so much," Callie whispered. She glanced at Eduardo out of the corner of her eye. He was standing back, watching them from the shadows.

"It's my fault." Pulling off his John Deere cap, her father rubbed his gray head with the heel of his hand. "I never should have written that nasty letter, chewing you out. It was just your Mom kept weeping, and you know I can't think straight when she's crying. I don't blame you for the silent treatment." His voice caught. "I wouldn't have written me back, either…"

Callie had no idea what he was talking about, but it felt so good to be with her family and have them clearly happy to see her and the baby. Marisol, looking at all the crying adults around her, gave a little worried whimper, looking up at Callie for reassurance. "It's all right," she told her, smiling. "It's finally all right."

As Jane Woodville held out her arms, tears were streaming down her plump cheeks and she looked like a slightly more wrinkled version of her granddaughter. "Can I hold her?"

The baby looked uncertain at first, but within sixty seconds, Jane had won her trust. Ten minutes later, Sami and then Grandpa Walter held her, and they heard Marisol's sweet baby giggle. Callie looked at her family, and could hardly believe that she'd been apart from them for seven months. They were the best, kindest people in the world.

Except for her husband. She looked at Eduardo adoringly, but he remained back in the shadows across the room.

"Mari-Marisol?" her father asked uncertainly.

Callie turned back, smiling through her tears. "Marisol Samantha Cruz."

"You named her after me?" Sami blurted out, her face screwed up with tears. "How could you forgive me? I was so selfish. I told myself calling your old boss was the right thing to do, but the truth is I didn't want you to marry Brandon." She sniffled. "How can you stand to look at me?"

"It *was* the right thing," Callie said through her tears. "Eduardo and I were meant to be together, and thanks to you we are. We're happy. Really happy…"

Callie looked back at Eduardo. He was still standing by the door, his arms folded as he watched the family reunion. Why didn't he come over to join them? It was strange. Any normal person would have come over to be part of the group. But Eduardo chose to be standoffish, to watch from a distance.

Her mother, standing beside her, followed her gaze.

"He loves you," Jane said softly.

Callie looked at her wistfully. "How can you tell?"

Jane smiled. "I see it in the way he looks at you. Like his

heart's nigh about to break." Reaching out, she squeezed her daughter's hand. "I still can't believe we're in Morocco. I always told your father that someday we'd travel and see the world. He said he'd do it as soon as it was free." She chuckled mischievously. "Eduardo's jet was the answer to my prayer."

The two women laughed, hugging each other, and for the rest of the afternoon, the family talked and giggled as Kasimir Xendzov's well-trained servants served refreshments and drinks. Eduardo continued to remain out of the circle, out of the group, until he finally disappeared all afternoon with his assistants to work on the deal. His behavior bewildered Callie. Was he just trying to give her some space with her family? But didn't he realize that he, too, was part of the family now?

After a delicious dinner of couscous and lamb, Callie said good-night to her jet-lagged parents and sister as they turned in to their luxurious bedrooms. After giving Marisol a bottle, she tucked her into a crib next door to their own large bedroom on the other side of the *riad* from the rest of her family. For the first time all day, Callie was alone. She looked at the large bed, covered with dark blue pillows. Fading sunlight fell upon the blanket in a pattern from the carved lattice window. She touched the bed. The mattress felt soft.

She heard a noise behind her. Jumping, she turned around.

Eduardo stood in the doorway. His eyes were dark, his expression set, as if braced for bad news.

"There you are," she said, furrowing her brow. "Where have you been? Why didn't you come talk to my family?"

"I didn't want to intrude."

Callie frowned, feeling puzzled by the strangeness of

his tone. She shook her head. "But you're part of our family now."

The door closed behind him as he came toward her in the bedroom. His voice was stilted. "Your family isn't rich."

She drew back, confused at the turn in conversation. "No. Especially not these days. My parents' farm has had a rough couple years...."

He came closer, something strangely intense in his dark eyes. "But you all still love each other."

"Of course we do," she said, bewildered. "Like you said—we're family."

His jaw twitched as he rubbed his wrist. In the shadowy bedroom, she saw the flash of his platinum watch. "Growing up, I thought money made a family. That it made people actually love each other enough to stay."

Callie's breath suddenly caught in her throat. "Money has nothing to do with it. Don't you know that?"

Eduardo gave her a tight smile.

"I'm glad you spent time with your family today. I have work to do before I meet with Xendzov tomorrow. Get some rest."

As he turned away, Callie stared after him, shocked. It was the first night she could remember when he hadn't wanted to accompany her to bed at night, to make love to her, to hold her until she slept.

He stopped at the door. "We need to talk," he said heavily. "Tomorrow. Then we'll see." He took a deep breath. "Afterward, I hope you will still…"

His voice trailed off. For a long moment, he stared at her, his eyes glittering in the shadows. Then he turned away, closing the bedroom door between them.

Callie was hardly able to sleep that night without him beside her. In the morning, she hurried down for breakfast, but he never appeared. She found out he'd left at dawn with his team of administrators and lawyers to work on the business deal with their invisible host, the mysterious Kasimir Xendzov. She thought it was strange, because Eduardo had seemed so determined to talk to her. About what?

And then she knew.

Was Eduardo finally going to tell her he loved her?

Joy filled her, followed by certainty. What else could it be? She was filled with happiness, counting down the moments until she'd see him again. She spent an enjoyable morning with her baby and family, sharing breakfast in the courtyard garden, walking around the estate, swimming in the pool. After lunch, as her parents took an afternoon nap with their grandbaby, Callie and Sami decided to explore the *souks* of Marrakech.

As the two sisters wandered the narrow, mazelike streets of the medina, Callie's heart was light. They walked through the outdoor markets, investigating booth after booth of copper lanterns, terra-cotta pots, embroidered *jellabas* and coral beads. She constantly checked her new cell phone in her handbag, just to make sure Eduardo hadn't called for her, but in the meantime, she was happy. Wearing a floppy pink hat, a billowy blouse and long skirt, with her wide-eyed sister at her side, Callie felt almost like a child again, when she and Sami went on "expeditions" across the wide fields and brooks of their family farm.

She suddenly froze in the middle of the outdoor market. Feeling prickles on her neck, as if someone was watching her, she whirled around.

But she only saw her bodyguard, Sergio Garcia, following at a discreet distance through the crowded medina. Eduardo never let her go anywhere without a bodyguard, and often more than one. Still, even as the afternoon passed and the hot Moroccan sun lowered to the west, the cold prickles on her neck didn't go away.

"So you really forgive me?" Sami asked softly.

Kneeling as she looked through a selection of copper lanterns, Callie smiled up at her sister. "I forgave you long ago—the day I named my daughter."

Sami's young face was dubious. "But if you forgave me, why didn't you write back?"

Callie straightened, frowning. "You wrote? When?"

"Lots of times! I even sent flowers! But other than the day Marisol was born, when you called us, we never heard a word. Not me, not Brandon, not even Mom and Dad!"

Callie gaped at her. "I wrote you letters every week! I sent hundreds of pictures!"

"We never got anything."

A shiver of ice went down Callie's spine. "Strange," she said faintly then tried to push it away with a smile. "But it doesn't matter anymore, does it?"

"We were worried about you," Sami said softly, clawing back her hair. "I'm glad you at least called us from the hospital when Marisol was born. Brandon arrived two days later and was so upset. He made it sound as if you'd been, well—" she bit her lip "—kidnapped."

Callie looked at her. "Have you been spending a lot of time with Brandon?"

Sami's cheeks turned pink. "Yeah."

"You're in love with him." It was a statement, not a question.

Sami stared at her then burst into tears. "I'm sorry," she whispered, wiping her eyes. "I've loved him for years." She tried to smile. "All the time that he loved you."

Callie shook her head. "I keep telling people—Brandon and I are just friends!"

Sami gave a hoarse laugh. "Man, you're dumb. Just as dumb as he was."

"*Was*? Have you told Brandon how you feel?"

"Not yet." Sami looked away. "I'm scared. We've spent a lot of time together lately, ice skating, looking at the stars, running errands. Whatever." She shivered beneath the fading afternoon sun of the Marrakech market. "Once, I almost thought he was going to kiss me. Then he turned away and started talking about you."

"He did?" Guilt went through Callie. "He must hate me."

"He hates Eduardo. Not you."

"Then why didn't he ever write me?" Callie whispered.

Sami looked at her as if she were crazy. "He did. I know he did. He showed me the letters."

The strange feeling went through Callie again, a dark cloud like a shadow over the sun. How was it possible that her family hadn't gotten any of her letters? Or that Callie hadn't gotten any of theirs?

Pushing the thought away, she turned back to Sami, putting her hand on her shoulder. She said firmly, "You should tell him how you feel."

Sami's eyes lit up then faded. "But what if he's not interested? What if he just laughs at me?"

"He won't."

"Yeah, but what if he does?"

"Life is short. Don't waste another day. Call him. Call him now."

"You're right." Sami stared at her then suddenly hugged her tight. "Thank you, Callie." Pulling away, she wiped her eyes. "I'll go back to the house. And call him in private. Oh," she breathed, wiping her shaking hands on her jeans, "am I really going to do this?"

"Sergio!" Callie called, wiping tears from her own eyes as she waved the bodyguard over. "Please take my sister back to the house."

"And you, Mrs. Cruz," Sergio Garcia said, his expression a smooth mask.

"I haven't finished my shopping."

"I can't leave you alone here, *señora*."

"I'll be fine," Callie said impatiently. She motioned to the busy *souk*. "There's no danger here!"

The bodyguard lifted an eyebrow. Turning away, he used his cell phone and spoke in low, rapid Spanish. Hanging up, he turned to Sami with a broad smile. "*Sí.* I can take you home, *señorita*."

"Thank you," Callie said, surprised. He'd never been so reasonable before. "Would you mind taking these bags back with you?"

"*Por supuesto, señora*." Garcia took her purchases, gifts for her parents, clothes and toys for Marisol, even a silver *koumaya* dagger for Eduardo. "Stay right here, Mrs. Cruz, in the open market."

"I will." Callie hugged her sister and whispered, "I think you and Brandon are perfect for each other."

"Thank you," Sami breathed fervently. "I love you, Callie." Then she was gone.

Callie was alone. She took deep breaths of the exotic, spicy scent of the air, of the distant leather tannery, of flowers and musky oriental perfumes. No bodyguard. No baby. Not even her husband. Callie was alone in this exotic foreign market. After so many months, the sudden freedom felt both disorienting and intoxicating.

Smiling to herself, she ignored the shouts of sellers trying to get her attention and walked through the market, feeling light as a feather on air as she continued to shop for gifts. Who knew if she'd ever return to Morocco again?

Her eye fell upon a tiny star carved in wood. It reminded her of Brandon's hobby that Callie found intolerably boring—astronomy. Thinking of him, a pang went through her.

Why didn't he ever write me?

He did. I know he did. He showed me the letters.

With a ragged breath, Callie lifted her gaze to the sky, turning toward the fading warmth of the sun. Above the busy, crowded, chaotic *souk*, a bird flew toward the distant Atlas Mountains. The setting sun had turned the snow-capped peaks a deep violet-pink.

"Callie."

She sucked in her breath. Slowly she turned.

Brandon McLinn stood in front of her.

Time slowed as he came toward her, tall and thin, standing out from the rest of the crowd in his cowboy hat, plaid flannel shirt and work-worn jeans. He stopped in front of her.

"At last," Brandon breathed, his eyes wet with tears. "I've found you."

"Brandon?" she whispered, her throat choking. "Is this a dream?"

"No." Smiling through his tears, he put a skinny hand on her shoulder. "I'm here."

"But what are you doing in Morocco?"

His hand tightened. "It took a miracle, all right," he said grimly. His eyes narrowed beneath his black-framed glasses. "No thanks to that Spanish bastard."

Callie gasped. "Don't call him that!"

He blinked, frowning. "But you hate him. Don't you? You said he was a playboy, that he had coal instead of a heart…that he couldn't be loyal to anything but his own fat bank account!"

Hearing her own words thrown back at her hurt. She

closed her eyes against her own cruelty. "He's not like that," she said over the lump in her throat. "Not really. He's—changed."

"Must be Stockholm Syndrome," Brandon snorted then his voice grew serious. "I've been so worried about you, Callie. I just let him take you away. I didn't save you."

Callie opened her eyes in shock. "*You* felt guilty?"

"I swore I'd leave no stone unturned, until you and your baby were back home. Safe, and free."

Smiling through sudden tears, she put her hand over his. "But we are safe. And free. I know our marriage had a rocky start, but he's been nothing but good to us."

"Good?" Brandon's jaw hardened. "He's had me followed for months."

"Followed?" she echoed.

"When Sami told me she was leaving for Marrakech, I skipped out in the middle of the night, slipping past the man watching my house. I drove to Denver and booked a flight. I've been staying at a hotel off this square, following your movements through Sami's messages."

"You knew I'd be at the market." Callie stared at him. "It was you I felt, watching me. Following us."

"Hoping to get you alone." He looked down at her, his eyes owl-like beneath his glasses. "I tried to contact you. Letters, phone calls. I tried everything short of a singing telegram. Last December, he called me in the middle of the night, warning me off. I threatened to call the police in New York. So he spirited you overseas. For the last four months, I had no idea where you even were!"

Callie remembered the night she'd caught Eduardo talking on the phone to a rival, he'd said, who lived far away. That very same night, he'd suddenly suggested they go to Spain. Once there, he'd never let her out of his sight, or even let her drive her own car, without a bodyguard. He'd said it was to keep her safe.

But safe from whom?

"I promised myself I wouldn't abandon you," Brandon said. "I've been waiting…praying…desperate. All the time he kept you prisoner."

Prisoner. Callie stared at him with a sick feeling in her belly. She was starting to think that Eduardo's planned talk later didn't involve him taking her in his arms and declaring his eternal love.

"I always knew the man was bad news." Brandon narrowed his eyes. "From the moment I first heard you talk about him. When he leased you that apartment in the Village, I knew he wanted you." His voice became bitter. "And from the sound of your voice, I knew you would let him."

"So you told Eduardo we were engaged," she said slowly. "The night he stopped by the apartment, you said…"

"I just told him the truth," he said stubbornly. "We *were* engaged. We said, if neither of us were married by the time we were thirty…"

"That was a joke!"

"It was never a joke to me." He looked down. "But I guess it was to you."

She stared at him, her cheeks aflame, unable to speak.

"I loved you, Callie," he said gruffly. "Since we were kids, I loved you."

She felt a lump in her throat, remembering their childhood. Chasing fireflies on warm summer nights. Watching fireworks on the Fourth. Christmas dinner with her cousins, aunts and uncles, turkey and stuffing and homemade pumpkin pie, sledding with her sister down McGillicuddy's hill. Even going out with Brandon's telescope at night and looking at stars until she wanted to claw her eyes out. It had been wonderful.

Her throat hurt. "I should have known. I'm sorry. But…I don't feel that way about you."

"Yeah. I figured that out." He took a deep breath then gave her a sudden crooked smile. "I've started to think that maybe I should look for someone who can love me. Who can see me. As more than a goofy, dependable friend."

Her heart broke a little in her chest. She tilted back her floppy pink hat. "Brandon—"

"But first I'm taking you and the baby home. We'll get you a good divorce lawyer. I don't care how much money Cruz has, the courts will see that you are in the right."

"You don't understand—"

"You don't have to be scared. We'll be with you every step of the way. Me. Your family—"

"I'm in love with him, Brandon," she blurted out. At his intake of breath, she lifted her eyes miserably. "I love him so much I think I might die of it. Every day all I can think is that I would do anything, absolutely anything, to make him love me back."

Brandon stared at her, his face pale. His Adam's apple bobbed then he looked at his feet as he said in a low voice, "I remember that feeling."

"I'm so sorry." Reaching out, she pulled him into her arms as she wept. "Forgive me."

For a moment, he accepted the comfort of her arms. They held each other, like kids dodging a storm.

"How can you love a man like that?" Brandon said in a low voice. "I accept that you can't love me. All right, fine. But a man who keeps you prisoner? Of all men on earth, you choose Cruz? A cruel, selfish beast of a man?"

Her heart lifted to her throat. "You don't know him,

Brandon. He's been hurt in the past. But he's not selfish and he's not cruel. If you only knew. He has such a good heart—"

Her voice ended in a gasp as Brandon was violently wrenched from her arms.

"Don't *touch* my wife!"

Turning in shock, Callie saw Eduardo's handsome face distorted with rage. A beam of blood-red light covered his black, civilized business suit, from the sun setting fire to the west.

"No, Eduardo, no!"

But he didn't hear her. Drawing back his fist, he punched Brandon so hard across the jaw that the other man, totally unprepared, dropped like a stone into the dust.

"No!" Callie shrieked. Around the *souk*, people stared at them across the busy, crowded market, speaking in a cacophony of languages. Fist raised, Eduardo started for Brandon again.

Callie ran between them, so fast her hat fell off her head. Holding up both her arms, she cried, "Don't!"

Eduardo whirled on her, his black eyes so hot that she should have burned to ash. "You told him to meet you here!"

"No, of course I didn't!" Looking at him, all Callie could suddenly think of was how he'd been lying to her face for months. How he'd caused her family pain. Forcing herself to take a deep, calming breath, she knelt down in the dust and checked on Brandon, who was knocked out cold but seemed otherwise fine. Rising to her feet, she glared at Eduardo. "Brandon couldn't contact me. A fact you know well."

Eduardo stared at her, breathing heavily. "What did he want from you?"

She lifted her chin. "To help me go back to North Dakota and file for divorce."

"And what did you say?"

"What do you think I said?" she cried. "I said no! Because I'm married to you. I have a child with you. I love you! Of course I told him no. Are you out of your mind?"

Baring his teeth, Eduardo grabbed her arm and pulled her away from the staring eyes of the *souk* and down the warren of streets to the parked car. Pushing her inside, he started the engine. It was only after they were back on the road that he spoke to her through gritted teeth.

"I found you in his arms."

Callie whirled on him. "I was comforting him!"

"I *trusted* you," he ground out.

"Trusted me?" She looked at him, tears in her eyes. "That's a joke! You never trusted me. You kept me a virtual prisoner, locked away from my family. Did you think I wouldn't find out?"

Eduardo looked at her, his handsome face pale beneath his tan. Setting his jaw, he didn't answer.

"When I think of all the time I spent," Callie whispered. "Sending them picture after picture, letter after letter." She looked up at him fiercely. "And the whole time, you were keeping them away, and me, locked away in your own little cage!"

He turned his eyes grimly back to the road. As he drove from the fortified gates of the medina toward the sprawling palm desert, he was silent, his jaw tight.

"You're not even trying to deny it," she said, tears streaming down her face.

He changed gears with more force than necessary. "I was going to tell you about it," he retorted. "It's why I told Sanchez he could leave you there. I wanted to surprise you at the market, and take you out to dinner just the two of us, so we could talk in private. So I could try to make you understand."

"I understand, all right!"

His hands clenched on the wheel. "I was trying to protect you. To protect all of us."

"Brandon said he was followed. Did you have me watched, too? What about my family?"

Eduardo looked at her then looked away.

"Keith Johnson had the detail," he said flatly.

The hot Moroccan air blew through the car window, whirling over her skin. "Keith Johnson?" she faltered. "But you use him to gain information on your rivals. On your enemies." She looked at him. "Which one am I?"

"You're my wife," he said tightly. "I was trying to keep you safe."

Her emotions were so jumbled she felt numb. "Safe!"

He glanced at her out of the corner of his eye. "What was I supposed to do?" he said roughly. "Let another man destroy our marriage?"

Callie's throat hurt. She closed her eyes, hearing the purr of the engine and soft whirr of the tires against the road.

"No," she whispered. "You destroyed it yourself."

She looked at him, and his dark eyes burned through her. Then wordlessly, he looked back at the road as the car turned into the gatehouse and drove up the sweeping entrance to the *riad*.

"We left Brandon," she cried. "Injured in the medina…"

"I'll send someone to check on him," Eduardo said coldly, not looking at her. "I wouldn't want your *best friend in all the world* to be left abandoned and alone."

Parking the car, he turned off the ignition and got out. Callie didn't move. She stared at the beautiful tile work of the grand home, at the green gardens and swaying palm trees above the blue-water pool. This place truly was paradise.

Her hands were shaking. She felt chilled to the bone.

The car door opened.

"Come, *querida*," Eduardo said quietly, reaching for her hand. She did not resist as he pulled her from the SUV and into the house. Inside the *riad*, all was quiet. Perhaps her parents and baby were sleeping. Callie heard only the soft burble of the fountain from the courtyard garden.

She felt her husband's hand in her own, as strong and protective around hers as it had ever been. But everything had changed. Was it only that morning that she'd been so happy, feeling like all her dreams were coming true? As Eduardo led her through the cloistered walk around the interior courtyard, she felt cold in the fading light of the sun.

"Why did you do it?" she rasped. "Why?"

Eduardo stopped.

"I'm tired, Callie," he said wearily. "Tired of trying to keep you. Tired of feeling like I'm failing. Tired of knowing, whatever I do, it won't be good enough."

"I did nothing but love you."

"Love is nice." His eyes glittered like hot coals as the edges of his lips curved. "Love changes nothing."

She stared at him, her heart chilled. "Is that what you think?"

"It's what I know," he said grimly, and that was the end. Her heart frosted over.

"You were right about one thing," she said. "Brandon was in love with me. But you've been so wrong about the rest. You are a wonderful father, Eduardo. But—" she gave him a trembling smile "—a terrible husband."

Hearing the noise of servants down the hall, he pulled her into their bedroom, closing the door behind them.

Looking down at her in the shadows, he spoke in a low voice.

"I always knew that someday you would see through me."

She felt trails of ice on her cheeks and lifted her hand to discover she was weeping. She loved him. But she wouldn't be his prisoner. Not anymore.

"I loved you, Eduardo." Her voice choked. "I loved you so."

His handsome face was hard with anguish. "*Loved*?"

"I would have done anything to make you love me," she whispered. "Anything." With a deep breath, Callie looked up at him through her tears. She squared her shoulders. "But I won't be your prisoner." Pulling off her diamond ring, she held it out to him with a trembling hand. "So I can't be your wife."

CHAPTER TEN

IT WAS like a punch through Eduardo's gut, a blow so deep it reverberated against his spine.

When he'd found Callie embracing McLinn, it had been like walking into a nightmare and seeing his worst fear come to life. He'd felt fury that he'd never known. He'd wanted to kill the man with his bare hands. And he might have done it, if not for Callie.

Now, sinking down on the bed, Eduardo stared at the ten-carat diamond ring twinkling in his palm. And realized that seeing Callie with another man had only been his *second*-worst fear.

Somehow, he'd always known this day would come. It was almost a relief to get it over with, rather than always wondering when it would happen. When she would leave him. His hands tightened over the ring, feeling the hard diamond bite into his palm. He spoke over the razor blade in his throat.

"I will start divorce proceedings tomorrow."

Her lips parted. "What?"

"I'll do what I should have done a long time ago." He looked at her. "Set you free."

Tears streaked her pale, beautiful face like stardust in the fading red twilight outside the latticed window. "I just can't live with a man who doesn't trust me. Who tries to control every aspect of my life."

"I understand." He gave her a grim smile. "I told you on our wedding day that when our marriage ended, the prenuptial agreement would see us through."

His wife looked white and wan, standing beside the bed. She looked like a ghost. "I didn't think you would let me go so easily."

He tried to ignore the fierce, white-hot blade of pain that entered his body.

"I am tired," he said harshly, "of always wondering what you're thinking. What you're doing. Tired of waiting for the day you'll wise up and leave." Rising to his feet, he cupped her cheek. She shuddered a little, turning toward his touch like a flower. He said hoarsely, "It's almost easier this way."

"And Marisol…" she whispered.

The knife twisted in his chest. Dropping his hand, he stepped back. "We will always be her parents. We'll be respectful of each other, for her sake. I will pay child support. We will share custody."

"Right," she said, looking dazed. "Right."

"And if there is another child…" His lips curved humorlessly. "This time, you will tell me, *sí*?"

"Yes. Yes, I will." Callie's lovely, round face looked bewildered as she swayed where she stood, like a drunk who'd lost her balance.

"You and your family can return to North America tomorrow."

She turned, walked two steps then looked back at him. He could see her shaking. "And Brandon?"

"Ah, yes." He smiled grimly. "Brandon. As you said, he is a member of your family, is he not? As I," he added lightly, "never was."

She swallowed then looked up at him pleadingly. "You won't…won't do anything to hurt him?"

Reaching out, Eduardo brushed some long wavy tendrils of light brown hair off her shoulder. Even now, saying goodbye, he was mesmerized by Callie's beauty. Now more than ever. When he was losing her forever.

"Of course I will not hurt him. I'm not the monster you seem to think." He remembered how he'd been tempted to kill the man just hours before, and shook his head with a hard laugh. "Well. I have no reason to hurt him now. Our marriage is over. We are free."

"Free…" she whispered.

McLinn's harsh words from long ago went through Eduardo's mind. *You can't keep me from her. We both know you're not good enough for her. You'll never make her happy.* And he realized that he'd always agreed. But he'd tried to keep Callie just the same. Selfish and wrong, when he knew he'd never be able to love her the way she deserved. Christ—he couldn't even sleep in the same bed.

"Yes. You're free." Eduardo turned away, making his voice deliberately casual as he said, "Marisol fell asleep in her playpen, in your parents' room. Do you want to see her?"

Callie did not answer. She just looked at him, her green eyes dark as a midnight sea. Her beautiful, grief-stricken face was more than Eduardo could bear. It had to end, he thought heavily. So let it end. Merciful and quick.

Taking his wife's limp hand, he pulled her out of their bedroom and through the deepening shadows of the courtyard. Midway through the garden, she stopped. He looked back at her in the twilight, surrounded by the shadows of palm trees and the soft cool burble of the fountain. Crystalline tears sparkled down her pale cheeks, glimmering in the fading moonlight.

"I'm sorry," she whispered, her eyes luminous. "So sorry."

Exhaling, Eduardo slowly pulled her into his arms. She pressed her face against his heart, which felt like it was breaking beneath his ribs.

Her voice was sodden, muffled against his shirt. "I didn't want it to end this way…"

His arms trembled around her. He thought of all his mistakes, everything he'd done wrong from the beginning, all the things he would have changed if he could. But the truth was he didn't know how. He couldn't trust anyone—especially not someone he loved. Because deep in his heart, he didn't believe in happy endings, only bad ones. Ones that felt like this.

"It was never your fault," he said, stroking her hair. "Just mine. All mine."

Hearing Callie sob, his throat constricted, and he wanted to cut out his ears, his eyes, rather than be faced with the pain he'd caused her. Desperately he pushed his feelings away, just as he'd done his whole life. Lifting her chin, he gave her a crooked smile. "Our marriage wasn't all bad, was it?"

"No," she whispered, searching his gaze in the shadows. "Most of it was wonderful."

"We gave our daughter a name. We will still give her a good home."

"Yes," she agreed. "But two homes. Apart."

He gave her a single unsteady nod then looked away, afraid of what she would see in his eyes. Afraid to speak and have her hear weakness in his voice. For long moments, he held her in the deepening shadows of the courtyard, listening to the water of the cool fountain as they stood in silence. Above them, palm trees waved against the deepening violet night.

Eduardo closed his eyes, breathing in the scent of her hair. Feeling the sweet softness of her body against his, knowing he was holding her for the last time.

It was best for her to leave. It was the only way to spare them both unnecessary pain. But the thought of it felt like death.

"It's all right," he said, gently brushing the tears from her cheeks, though he knew it would never be all right again. "You'll go home. You'll be happy there, just like you were."

"Yes, I will." She wept.

He heard the hoarseness of her voice, and knew what the words cost her. Emotion rushed through him, and before he could stop himself, he cupped her face in both his hands. "But before you leave, there's one thing you have to know. One important thing I've never said." He looked down at her. "I love you."

Callie sucked in her breath, her eyes wide.

"I love you as I've never loved anyone." He looked down at the flowers at his feet. "But I can't love you without hurting you. Without hurting both of us. Without being a man I don't want to be." Looking at her stricken face, he whispered over the razor blade in his throat, "That's why I'm letting you go."

In the shadows of the garden, Callie's eyes were deep emerald, like an ancient forest older than time itself. Her beauty was like an ache in his heart. Unwillingly he lifted his hand to her cheek, touching the softness of her skin as he looked into her eyes, connecting them soul to soul. Beneath the violet-tinged sky swept with stars, he heard the howl of the wind, shaking the palm trees above.

"I'm sorry I couldn't love you as you deserve," he said hoarsely. "I always knew I didn't deserve you. And I knew, from the beginning, that it was a matter of time—"

Standing on her toes, Callie cut off his words by covering his mouth with her own.

Her lips were soft and sweet, trembling against him. He felt the warmth of her body against his, and a surge of anguished need rushed through him like an overflowing river. A gasp came from the back of his throat, and he wrapped his arms around her, pulling her against him tightly as he returned her kiss hungrily. On her lips, he tasted salt with the sweet and no longer knew if they were her tears, or his own. All he knew was that he was kissing her for the last time and he had to make it last forever. He had to kiss her so deep and hard that he'd possess this memory for all time, not just on his lips, but in his heart.

Eduardo's fingers twined through her long hair as they embraced, their bodies pressing together as they clutched each other mindlessly in front of the courtyard fountain. He felt the tangled smoothness of her hair, breathed in her scent of flowers and vanilla that mingled with the exotic spices of the desert wind. He stroked down her back, marveling at her shape as he wrapped his far larger body around the small woman who'd conquered him so completely. Looking at her, touching her soft skin, feeling her breasts against his chest, he kissed her with anguished passion. Need burned away every other thought or desire of his soul, except to possess her.

With a gasp, he pulled away. Looking down at her beautiful face, he saw the shadows of the rising moon move against her skin; saw the breathless, aching need in her eyes. Without a word, he lifted her up into his arms. He carried her silently to their bedroom.

For the last time, he took Callie to bed.

Setting her down on the mattress, beneath the pattern of moonlight through the latticed window, Eduardo pulled off her blouse, kissing her neck, her shoulders, her arms.

He pulled off her skirt, stroking the length of her legs, kissing the sensitive spot behind her knees with a flick of his tongue. He pulled off her lacy white bra, cupping her breasts, suckling her until she gasped.

"Callie," he said hoarsely. "Look at me."

She obeyed, and her beautiful eyes shimmered with tears as she watched him move down her body, pulling her panties down her legs. Still fully dressed in his black suit, he kissed her naked body. Up her calves. Her inner thighs. He paused at the crux of her thighs, letting the warmth of his breath curl between her legs, inhaling the tantalizing scent of her.

Pushing her thighs apart with his hands, he bent his head and tasted her, stretching her wide. She was sweet and smooth as satin. He nestled himself between her thighs and flicked the tip of his tongue against her hard, aching core. He felt her writhe beneath him, bucking her hips to escape the intensity, so he held her hips against the bed, forcing her to accept the full rough pleasure of his tongue. He stroked her, lapped her. When she was dripping wet and trembling, he pushed three fingers a single inch inside her.

Panting for breath, she threw out her hands, gripping the soft cotton blankets as he suckled her hard pink nub, swirling his tongue in featherlight circles and pressing his fingers deeper and deeper inside her. Callie's hands tightened on the blankets, her back arching, as if only her grip kept her from flying off the bed. He heard the long gasp of her breath, felt her body lifting from the mattress, higher, higher, felt her body grow tense and tenser still. Until she exploded.

Her soft, wet walls contracted tightly around his fingers as she cried out, twisting her body from side to side, in a symphony of mindless, helpless pleasure. He watched her face. He'd given her that pleasure. He'd made her weep with grief. But at least he'd also made her scream with joy. As she opened her eyes, still panting for breath, her expression was almost bewildered as she looked up at him. "I love you," she whispered.

Cupping her face, he looked down at her. "I know."

She stroked his face, his hair, his neck, his jacket. He lowered her mouth to hers, and she kissed him back almost savagely. He felt her tongue, her teeth. He felt her need for him. He felt her heart. Fully dressed, he moved against her, his erection hard and throbbing against her thighs.

A sob come low from her throat. She flung her arms around his neck, pulling him down against her with sudden desperation. Her fingers frantically attempted to pull off his tie, to unbutton his shirt. Pulling away from her, he yanked off his coat and tie. He ripped his civilized white shirt and tailored trousers and silk boxers to the cool tile floor.

Naked, he faced her, his soul as bare as his body. Without a word, he lowered his mouth to hers, stroking her, telling her with his touch everything he could not trust himself to put into words.

Covering her body with his own, he felt her full breasts against his chest, felt her soft, feminine curves sway against his hardness. The satin-smooth skin of her inner thighs stroked the hard length of his shaft, and her wet core tantalized his aching tip alluringly. He heard her gasp with need as she twisted her body beneath him, gripping his hips with her hands, trying to pull him closer, spreading her thighs in unconscious seduction.

But he did not want to take her. No. Not yet. Beads of sweat covered his forehead as he held himself apart from everything he wanted most. This was the last time he would possess her, and he wanted to make it last forever. As long as she was in his arms, he would not have to face the heartbreak and grief that waited for him on the other side. He would not have to face the dark solitude without her…

She stroked his back, her breasts plumping against his chest. He felt the sweaty heat of her skin, heard the breathless hush of her sigh. Gripping her shoulders, he closed his eyes, trying to resist. But she knew him too well. She moved beneath him, suckling his earlobe, breathing on his neck as she ran her hands on the back of his upper thigh, below his buttocks, between his legs. She stroked him—and he felt the hot, wet core of her slide against him—pulling him inside—

With a choked gasp, he surrendered. His body took over. With a low growl, he grabbed her shoulders and plunged himself inside her in a single deep thrust. Her body tensed, then melted, parting for him, accepting him, embracing every inch of his thick length. Pulling back, he thrust again with a gasp, and again, riding her. His every muscle was taut in the exquisite precipice between agony and pleasure. Six thrusts and only the grimmest vestige of self-control kept him from exploding inside her. But he had to make it last. He had to. He could not live without her.…

Rolling onto his back, he lifted her over him, impaling her. Her thighs gripped his hips as he let her control the rhythm and speed. After months of bed play, his once-virgin secretary had become a fiery seductress. He thought having her on top would slow him down, make him last. But instead, as she pushed herself against him, he filled her harder and deeper than he ever had. Her heavy breasts swayed back and forth against his face as she rode him, going deeper with each thrust, until he closed his eyes, panting beneath the brutal onslaught of pleasure. Reaching his hands behind him, he gripped the headboard of the bed.

Harder, deeper. And wet, so wet. As she slammed

against him, her walls wrapped around him, tight, so tight, pulling him into an abyss of mindless pleasure. His eyes rolled back as he gripped her hips with his hands, his whole body shaking with the agony of need. He felt her quicken and pulse around him as she flung back her head and screamed with joy. Looking up at her, seeing her beautiful face filled with ecstasy, her eyes closed as if in prayer, he could no longer resist. With one last savage thrust he exploded inside her, riding the wave with her. His hoarse cry mingled with hers as he came and came and came, never looking away from her beautiful face.

And Callie collapsed on top of him, clutching him to her hot, sweaty body, happiness pouring out of them both like radioactive light.

Afterward, Eduardo held her. For the first time, he was grateful knowing that he wouldn't be able to sleep beside her. He could hold her all night. He'd watch her gentle face slumber beneath the latticed moonlight. She felt so soft in his arms. So warm. So sweet. His eyelids became heavy as he held her. Closing his eyes, he kissed her temple, breathing in the vanilla and floral scent of her hair. He loved her so much he thought he could die of it. He would hold her all night long. He'd relish every hour. Every minute…

Eduardo woke with a gasp.

The pink light of morning poured in through the window as he realized that he'd slept beside his wife for the first time.

In panic, he looked at her side of the bed.

It was empty. For the first time, Callie had been the one to rise in the middle of the night. She'd been the one to leave. And as the first wave of anguish hit his body, he knew this was how he'd always known he would be.

Alone.

CHAPTER ELEVEN

CALLIE sat at the kitchen table of her parents' farmhouse and looked at the papers in her shaking hands. The words seem to swim in front of her eyes.

Divorce papers.

"It'll be quick and painless," her lawyer had assured her when he'd given her the file. "I marked each place for you to sign with a yellow tab. All the tough questions were already dealt with in the prenup. You'll share custody, switching visitation each week, and with Mr. Cruz's extremely generous level of alimony and child support you'll be the richest woman in Fern County." The lawyer gave her a sudden sharp grin. "Good thing every divorce case isn't so quick and painless, or else I'd be bankrupt."

Quick. Painless. Callie heard a wheel squeak as her nine-month-old daughter crossed the floor in the antique walker used by three generations of Woodville babies. Marisol giggled at the sound, and her laughter was like music. Callie smiled at her daughter through her tears.

"Pa-pa-pa?" Marisol said hopefully.

Callie's smile faded as she looked down at the papers. "Soon, sweetheart," she said over the lump in her throat. "You'll see him tomorrow." Marisol would be flown back to New York for a week with Eduardo, and Callie would have to endure seven long, aching days without her child.

Then the next week, they would switch, and it was Eduardo who would be alone.

He'd been fair. More than fair, allowing Callie to live at such a distance, using his private jet to shuttle Marisol between North Dakota and New York. Callie had no idea what they'd do when it was time for Marisol to start school, but something would surely be worked out. Money, it seemed, could solve any problem.

Except this.

Callie didn't want his money. She wanted him. She was still in love with him.

But he'd let her go.

She hadn't seen Eduardo for two months, since she'd left Marrakech with her baby, Brandon and her family. Since then, their only point of contact had been through their lawyers. Even Marisol's pickups and drop-offs each week were handled by Mrs. McAuliffe.

Callie hadn't seen him. But each night, she dreamed of him, of their last night together, when they'd kissed in the shadows by the fountain. When they'd made love so passionately and desperately the bed seemed to explode into fire. When he'd huskily spoken the words she still, against her will, held to her heart.

I love you. I love you as I've never loved anyone. But I can't love you without hurting you.

Once, she would have given ten years of her life to hear Eduardo say he loved her. Now, the words were poison. She'd cried for weeks, till there were no tears left. But there was no other answer. She couldn't live as his prisoner. And he couldn't risk giving her his heart if she wasn't.

Two teardrops fell on the divorce papers spread out across her parents' blue Formica table. When she'd come back home, part of her had hoped she might be pregnant, which would at least give her a reason to talk to her husband again. But even that hope had failed her.

"Ma-ma?" Marisol's dark eyes, exactly like her father's, looked up at her mother with concern.

"It's all right," Callie whispered, wiping her eyes and giving her daughter a tremulous smile. "Everything is fine." All she had to do was sign the papers and her lawyer would file them. She'd be Callie Woodville again. Callie Cruz would disappear.

Across the small kitchen, where it sat in a small woven basket, the gold and diamond double "CC" key chain flashed at her in the morning light. It seemed forlorn and out-of-place in the key basket, amid the clutter of pens, sticky notes and unpaid utility bills around the twenty-year-old phone. But even her keychain wasn't as out-of-place as the shipment that had arrived at their rural North Dakota farm yesterday. Picking up her steaming mug of coffee, Callie went to the kitchen window and pushed aside the red gingham curtain.

Outside, beside her father's red, slightly rusted 1966 pickup truck, her sleek silver car was now parked in front of the barley field.

Callie closed her eyes. She'd never thought she would have the strength to leave Eduardo.

But then, she never thought he'd let her go.

And he'd already moved on. She'd already seen pictures of Eduardo in a celebrity magazine, attending a charity gala in New York with the young Spanish duchess. Callie wondered if they'd marry, once his divorce to her was final. Her heart twisted with jagged pain at the thought, and for the first time, she truly understood what Eduardo must have felt when he'd thought she was in love with Brandon.

How hard it was, to set the person free that you loved most on earth. But Eduardo had done it.

Now so must she.

Callie heard an engine coming up the long driveway. Looking back out the window, she smiled. About time. Taking another sip of her coffee, Callie watched Brandon and Sami leap out of the Jeep.

Brandon's heart hadn't remained broken for long. Since their return from Morocco, now freed of his guilt and concern over Callie, he'd finally allowed himself to give his heart to the young woman who'd been his constant companion for nine months. Yesterday, he'd asked Sami to marry him.

Their parents had been cautious at first, then ecstatic. News of the engagement had rapidly spread across Fern, and thanks to Jane's eager posting, to all her internet friends, across the world. Callie swallowed, feeling a little misty-eyed. *Engaged.* Her best friend and little sister were planning to be married in September.

As the two vagabonds traipsed through the door, Callie shook her head with a wry laugh. "Engaged or not, sis, Mom and Dad are not happy you stayed out all night."

"It was totally innocent!" Brandon protested. Then his full cheeks blushed beneath his black-framed glasses as he gave Sami a sudden wicked grin. "Well, *mostly* innocent…"

"We were up at McGillicuddy's Hill," Sami said quickly, "to see the comet away from the lights. There were so many stars." She looked dreamily at her fiancé. "Brandon knows all the constellations. We just lost track of time…"

"Good luck explaining that to Dad."

"Dad knows he can trust Brandon," she protested. She turned to him. "Like I do. With my life."

Brandon looked back at Sami with love in his eyes. Taking her hand in his own, he kissed it fervently. And Callie suddenly felt like an intruder, standing in the cozy, warm kitchen in her old purple sweatpants and ratty T-shirt. "All right," she said awkwardly. "You should talk to him, though."

"Where is he? Out in the fields?"

Callie nodded. "Alfalfa by the main road."

"Don't worry." Brandon clutched Sami's hand. "You won't have to face him alone."

"I know."

As he pulled his car keys out of his pocket, they turned toward the door. On impulse, Callie blurted out, "Wait."

They paused, staring at her questioningly. Crossing to the key basket, Callie took the "CC" keychain and held it out to them. "I want you to have this."

"What?" Sami exclaimed. "Your car?"

Brandon glowered. "Why?"

"It's—" Callie grasped at straws "—an engagement gift."

"Are you kidding?" Sami blurted out.

"We don't need anything from *him*." Brandon looked mutinous. It was possible he still nursed a grudge. "My Jeep works just fine."

Sami turned to him. "Think of it as compensation for him punching you," she said hopefully.

It didn't help her case. Brandon scowled.

"Please take it." Callie shook her head. "I hate looking at it. It makes me remember…" Her voice trailed off, as she felt overwhelmed by sweet memories of the Christmas day Eduardo had dressed in a Santa suit and given it to her. How happy they'd been… She gave them a tremulous smile. "Sell it. Use the money however you like."

The young couple looked at the dangling gold-and-diamond keychain.

"We could buy land," Sami said.

"A farm of our own," Brandon breathed. He blinked then snatched the keychain from her hand. "Very well. We accept." He paused, tilting his head with a grin. Then he sobered. "Thanks, Callie. Thanks for being the best friend I've ever had." He turned to Sami. "Till now."

And then they were gone, racing out of the farmhouse to the car parked near the barn. Their conversation floated back to Callie on the June breeze.

"One ride before we sell it?"

"Let's go the long way, past the Coffee Stop!" Sami giggled. "I want to see Lorene Doncaster's face when she sees me in this thing…."

"Your father will forgive us for being out all night. I'll explain. It was the fault of the stars…"

The fault of the stars. Alone in the kitchen, Callie stood in the warm sunlight of her mother's cheerful kitchen. She looked back at the divorce papers. She saw the black, angular scrawl of Eduardo's signature. He'd asked for a divorce. It was the only thing to do.

Wasn't it?

She picked up the pen in her trembling hand. She looked down at the empty line beneath his black signature.

Was their marriage really nothing more than a nine-month mistake?

She exhaled, closing her eyes.

Then, an hour later, she got a call that changed everything.

"Good progress today. So, same time next week?"

Eduardo nodded, pulling on his jacket. He left the therapist's office and took a deep breath of the morning air. The June sky was bright blue over Manhattan.

"Sir?" Sanchez stood ready at the curb, waiting beside the black Mercedes sedan.

Eduardo shook his head. "Think I'll walk."

"Very well, sir."

Eduardo walked slowly down the street, feeling the sun on his face, hearing the birds sing overhead. A bunch of laughing schoolkids in identical uniforms ran by him on the sidewalk, reminding Eduardo of the *Madeline* book he'd read to his two-week-old daughter, to the great amusement of his wife.

He stopped, feeling a sudden pain in his chest.

He would see Marisol soon, he reminded himself. His jet was already gassed up and ready at a private airport outside the city. He glanced at his platinum watch. Mrs. McAuliffe was likely headed for the airport now, if she wasn't there already, preparing to make the long flight across the country and back. She would collect the baby from his soon-to-be ex-wife. From the woman who still haunted his dreams.

Blankly Eduardo stared up at the green trees above the sidewalk. The trees looked exactly like they had in early September, when he'd first shown up in the West Village demanding marriage. On the day when, in the space of a few hours, he'd gained both a wife, and a child.

His stomach clenched. He suddenly couldn't bear the thought of going back to work. All those hours of work, all those days and years, and for what? He was a billionaire, and yet he envied his chauffeur, who went home every night to a snug little home in Brooklyn with a wife who loved him and their three growing children. Eduardo had a huge penthouse on the Upper West Side filled with art and expensive furniture, but when he was alone, the hallways and rooms echoed with the laughter of his baby. Of his lost wife.

Soon to be *ex*-wife.

He clenched his hands into fists. Had Callie signed the papers yet? Why hadn't she signed them?

It had been two weeks since he'd signed the divorce

papers, and the waiting was slowly driving him mad. He wanted it done, finished. Every day he was still married to Callie was acid on his heart, making him question if he'd made a mistake, if there was still a chance she might have forgiven him—if he could have earned back her trust.

He clawed his hair back with his hand. No. No way. She was probably engaged to Brandon McLinn by now and planning their wedding. McLinn's steadfast loyalty had triumphed at last. And unlike Eduardo, McLinn fit into Callie's world as Eduardo never would. He'd remember to ask her father for permission first. No one could ever deserve Callie, but if anyone had earned her, it was Brandon McLinn.

So why hadn't she signed the papers? Why?

He didn't know. He honestly didn't know. And it was like crossing a high-wire without a net.

Since Callie had left him in Marrakech, he hadn't checked up on her once. He'd fired Keith Johnson from her case. He'd even given his lawyers strict instructions not to give him news of her. They were to contact Eduardo when her lawyer had filed the signed paperwork for the divorce, and not before.

But he still hadn't got the call. Did that mean there was hope?

Closing his eyes, Eduardo turned his face toward the sun as he thought about how he'd isolated her during their marriage. No. No hope.

"Hey!"

Looking down, Eduardo saw a little girl of about eight or nine, standing apart from five other schoolgirls. She held up a picture. "You dropped this."

Reaching out, he took the photo of Callie and Marisol, taken at the Spanish villa at Christmas. Marisol was just three and a half months old then, giggling, flashing her single tooth. Callie was mischievously wearing the Santa hat she'd stolen from Eduardo, smiling as he took the picture. Her green eyes glowed with love. Grief choked him, so much his knees nearly went weak. "Thanks."

"I know how it feels to lose things," the little girl said. "Don't be careless."

He looked up, his eyes wide.

"See ya." With a skip, the girl turned away, racing back down the street with her friends, with the reckless joy of childhood freedom.

And a lightning bolt hit his heart.

Eduardo had told Callie to leave. He'd been the one who'd filed for divorce. He'd set her free, knowing she deserved better than a man who tried to control her, to spy on her, who wouldn't trust her.

But what if he could have just chosen to be a different man?

Eduardo stared at the flow of traffic on the busy street. What if his past didn't have to infect his future? What if he could choose a different life?

Hope rose like a wave inside his soul, no longer to be repressed. He'd set Callie free. But could he do the same for himself—be the man he wanted to be? The divorce wasn't final yet. Was there still time?

Could he ask her for a second chance?

Ask her to be his wife—not his prisoner, but his partner?

Gripping the photo, he whirled around, causing four construction workers to spit curses as he knocked past them on the sidewalk. Eduardo caught up with Sanchez just as his sedan was pulling from the curb. Yanking open the back door, Eduardo threw himself inside. "The airport!" he panted. "I need to see my wife—now!"

Sanchez gave him an enormous smile. "Yes, sir!"

He stomped on the gas, and Eduardo pulled out his phone to call Mrs. McAuliffe about the change in plans. Before he could, his phone rang in his hand. He saw Keith Johnson's number. Scowling, he turned the sound to Mute. But after he hung up with Mrs. McAuliffe, as the car crossed the George Washington Bridge, his phone buzzed again. Looking down, he saw his lawyer's number and a chill went down his spine.

His lawyer.

Did that mean…

Could it be…

Eduardo narrowed his eyes. No. As the phone stopped, then urgently started to vibrate a second time, Eduardo rolled down the window, and tossed it into the Hudson.

It wasn't too late for him to change. He wouldn't let it be.

He made it to the airport as his jet was warming up, and took his place on the jet bound for North Dakota. Refusing his surprised flight attendant's offer of his usual martini, Eduardo paced back and forth across the cabin for hours, planning what he would say to Callie. He tried to write down his feelings then finally gave up in disgust. He would pray that once he saw her, he'd know what to say.

Sitting restlessly in the white leather seat by the window, he felt like a jangle of nerves. Wishing the jet could go faster, he looked down through the wispy clouds and watched the green rolling hills of the East Coast slowly transform to the flat, brownish landscape of the northern prairies.

When they finally landed at the tiny airport outside of Fern, his legs were shaking as he went down the steps to the tarmac. The airport was just like he remembered when he'd visited so long ago, the day Callie had come to meet him as the local office liaison. But this time, he had no staff. He was alone.

Eduardo had forgotten what it was like to exist without layers of employees and servants insulating him from the real world. He felt clumsy, trying to remember how to do things himself, with no assistants. No bodyguards. On impulse, he stopped at the airport's single shop to buy Callie some flowers and an eight-dollar box of chocolates. The place was deserted, and it took five long minutes before the salesclerk even noticed he was there, and came out from the back to ring up his order.

But Eduardo didn't chew him out. He didn't try to throw his weight around. He no longer wanted to rule this town. He wanted to fit in. He was suddenly desperate to be part of Callie's world, if only she would let him.

He didn't go completely unnoticed. At the car rental counter, the female clerk looked at his face, then his credit card. Her jaw fell open, and her gum almost fell out of her mouth.

"Eduardo Cruz?" she said faintly. "*The* Eduardo Cruz? The owner of Cruz Oil?"

"Don't hold it against me." Impatient as he was to find Callie, he gave her his best attempt at a grin. "I, um, seem to have lost my phone. Do you happen to know the way to the Woodville farm? Walter and Jane Woodville's place?"

"Of course I know it." The young woman chewed her gum thoughtfully. "At the corner of Rural Route 12 and Old County Road. I went to school with their daughter." Her eyes darkened. "I saw her driving around in the Rolls-Royce yesterday…."

"Thank you. She's the one I came to see—"

"But she's not at home," she said. "I'm sorry to tell you this if you're a friend, but she was in an accident. A car accident."

Eduardo nearly staggered back. "What?"

"That car was smashed right up," she said sadly.

Car accident. Memories went through him of when he'd heard of his mother's death in a smash-up on a treacherous road on the Costa del Sol. An icicle of stark fear went down his spine. "You are mistaken," he said faintly. "That car is very safe...."

"Some kids were riding bicycles in the middle of the road. Her fiancé swerved, and the car smashed straight into a telephone pole. She's in critical condition at County General...."

Eduardo reached across the counter, his eyes wild. "Who's her fiancé? Who is he?"

"Brandon McLinn…"

He didn't wait to hear more. He grabbed a map off the counter.

"Mr. Cruz, I really am sorry—"

Running to his rental car, he drove for the hospital, racing down the highway at a hundred miles an hour. If he got pulled over by a policeman, he knew he'd go to jail. But he didn't give a damn.

He couldn't lose her. Not now...

Anguish gripped his throat. He could have been with her all this time. He could have been chasing her the last two months, trying to make her forgive him, trying to be the man she deserved. Instead he'd let her go. Why couldn't he have just treated her right from the beginning? Why had he wasted so much time trying to control their lives? Control was the illusion, not love. There was no such thing as perfect safety. No such thing as perfect control. You couldn't make someone love you. And even if you did, you couldn't make it last forever.

People left. People died.

But love endured. He could choose to love Callie with

all his heart and strength, love her with full knowledge of both her flaws and his own; love her with every ounce of his being until the day he died. That was his choice.

He'd once told her that love changed nothing. It was wrong. It changed everything.

Clutching the steering wheel, he prayed he'd reach her in time. Callie had to be all right. His daughter couldn't grow up without a mother. He couldn't live without his wife.

The afternoon sunlight cast the waving fields in a golden glow beneath the wide blue skies. He increased his speed to a hundred and twenty, as fast as the little rental car would go along the empty highway.

Don't leave me, Eduardo begged soundlessly. *Don't leave me.*

CHAPTER TWELVE

IT HAD been a horrible night. And a very long day.

Callie rose achingly from the chair by her sister's hospital bed. She needed coffee or fresh air. She was still wearing the same purple sweatpants and T-shirt from yesterday, with her hair pulled back in a ponytail. They'd all been awake through the night, and now, in late afternoon, everyone had collapsed with exhaustion. Brandon was curled up in a chair on the other side of Sami's bed, and Jane and Walter had fallen asleep on the couch, her mother's head on her father's shoulder, and baby Marisol snoring loudly against her grandpa's chest.

Callie quietly left the hospital room. Once she was safely in the hallway, she took a deep breath and sagged back against the door, covering her face with her hands. It was all her fault. If she hadn't given them the car they wouldn't have taken the detour through town. They wouldn't have been in the accident.

Tears burned Callie's eyes. But the crisis was past. Her sister would recover.

She was grateful beyond measure, but the tears weren't just out of gratitude. Callie had a good reason to feel an extra dose of anguish today. A private reason of her own...

She closed her eyes. She missed Eduardo so much. His handsome face. His glowing dark eyes. And his voice. She could almost hear it now, rough with an edge of Spanish accent.

"Where's my wife? Where is she, damn you?" The man's voice echoed down the hallways of the small hospital. "I want to see her *now*!"

She knew that voice. She still dreamed about it every night. Slowly Callie turned.

And saw Eduardo arguing at the nurses' station down the hall. His black hair was rumpled, and so was his suit. She'd never seen him so disheveled before, so completely out-of-place, so handsome and powerful and everything she'd ever wanted.

"Eduardo," she choked out.

At the end of the hall, he turned and saw her. With a sob, she started toward him at a run, in the same instant he started running for her.

They fell into each other's arms, and it was only when Callie actually felt him, strong and solid beneath her hands, that she knew for sure it wasn't a dream. She felt his protective, steadying arms around her and all the fear and shock of the last twenty-four hours fell away. She no longer had to be strong for her family. She burst into tears.

"Callie, Callie," he whispered fervently, kissing her forehead. "You're all right. Thank God, you're all right."

Pulling back, he looked down at her, his eyes glistening suspiciously in the hospital's fluorescent lights. Then he wrapped his powerful arms around her tightly, holding her as if he never wanted to let her go. Callie exhaled for the first time in two months, weeping with the joy of being again in his arms.

"You're safe," he breathed, stroking her hair as she pressed her face against his chest. "Safe."

Wiping her eyes, she looked at him in confusion. "But

what are you even doing here? I thought you were in New York?"

"Would you believe me if I said I was in the neighborhood?"

She smiled weakly.

"I, um, brought you some flowers and candy." Looking around, he cursed softly. "They are here somewhere…"

"Oh. Right." Her heart dropped. With all the worry about her sister's accident, she'd forgotten his week started today. She said dully, "You're here for Marisol."

Eduardo stared at her, his dark eyes infinite and deep as the ocean. "I'm here for you." He took her hands in his own. "Come back to me, Callie. Give me one more chance."

"What?" she breathed.

"Be my wife. Let me be your partner, by your side. Let me spend the rest of my life loving you. And striving to deserve your love in return."

Her voice caught in her throat. "I…"

He gave her an unsteady smile. "I'm too late, aren't I?"

"Too late?"

He looked past her ear. "You've moved on."

Turning around, she saw Brandon peeking out of her sister's door, his face questioning before he ducked back. Frowning, Callie turned back at Eduardo. "What are you talking about?"

"The girl at the car rental counter told me about your accident. She also told me that you're engaged. You and Brandon." His eyes were bleak as he tried to smile. "I guess I should offer my congratulations."

Callie nearly staggered back with shock.

"You don't know," she whispered. Sudden rising joy filled her heart, choking her with hope. "The engagement announcement was on my mom's web page days ago. It was even in the newspaper this morning. But *you don't know.*"

Eduardo shook his head, his jaw tight, his eyes forlorn. "I fired my investigator two months ago. Told my lawyers not to talk about you. I even threw away my phone."

"Your *phone*?"

"I was mad at it." He gave her a small smile. "I still do some stupid things. But my therapist says there's hope…"

"Your therapist!" she cried, nearly falling over in shock.

"Talking about the past has helped me understand the choices I've made as an adult. And why I was so afraid to love you." He took a deep breath. "Because I do love you, Callie. So much." He looked down at the green cracked tiles of the floor. "Brandon is…he is a good man. I know he'll make you happy."

Moving closer, she reached up and lifted his chin. "Brandon and I aren't together. He's engaged to my sister."

Slowly Eduardo lifted his head. Shock filled his expression, followed by savage joy. "Your sister?"

"I gave them the car yesterday and she was hurt in the crash." She pressed her lips together. "We were worried. For a few hours last night the doctors weren't sure she'd make it. She lost a lot of blood. But she came out of surgery this morning and the doctors say she'll be fine. She just needs a lot of rest."

"Thank God." He hugged her close and whispered, "So she's engaged to Brandon. I always knew I liked her."

She pressed her cheek against his shirt, and her tears made the fabric wet as she sniffled. "Ever since it happened, all I could think about was that I wished you were here. So you could hold me and tell me that everything would be all right."

"Oh, *querida*." For a long moment, he held her tightly then he looked down at her. "I know I'm selfish and ruthless and occasionally a jerk. There will be times in the future you'll want to punch me. But give me one more chance to love you. Just say the word," he vowed, "and I will never again leave your side."

She started to speak, but he put his finger to her lips. "Before you give your answer," he whispered, "let me finish my argument…."

Lowering his mouth to hers, he kissed her in an embrace so pure and breathless and true that it left her in no doubt of his love for her, and so passionate it left her dizzy and swaying in his arms.

She looked up at him.

"Stay with me, Eduardo," she breathed, blinking back tears. "Don't ever go."

His dark eyes lit up with joy. "Callie—"

"I love you," she whispered, and he kissed her again, so long and hard that several members of the hospital staff cleared their throats and made loud comments suggesting they *get a room* before Eduardo finally pulled away.

"I wish I'd done things differently from the start," he said against her hair. "That I'd given you a real wedding, and asked your father for your hand…" He snorted, his eyes twinkling as he confessed, "Do you know I actually tried to write you a poem on the flight here?"

"You did?"

"A love poem."

"A love poem from the great Eduardo Cruz." Giggling, Callie shook her head. "Now that is something I really, really want to read."

"Not in this lifetime. You'd laugh yourself silly."

"I could do with a laugh." Callie put her hand on his hard, rough cheek, then slowly traced down his throat, to linger against his chest. "And we both know you'll give it to me sooner or later."

She felt him shiver beneath his touch. "Yes," he said huskily. "I will." He took a deep breath as he cupped her face. "I will give you everything. Everything I have. Everything I am. Both the good and bad."

"For better or for worse." Rising on her tiptoes, she kissed him again, in clear and complete defiance of the hospital staff. She felt the hard, satin strength of his lips, felt the heat of his tongue brush against her own. She wanted to kiss him forever. And she could. She was his wife....

Callie pulled back with a horrified gasp, her eyes wide.

"What is it, *querida*?"

"I signed the divorce papers yesterday!" she wailed. She gave a choked sob as she threw her arms around him. "Oh, Eduardo. We're divorced!"

He blinked then slow joy lifted his handsome features, like the rise of the first spring dawn after endless cold winter. He gave a low laugh. Lifting her chin, he stroked her tears away with the pads of his thumbs. "Oh, my love. That's the best news you could have given me."

She blinked in shock. "It—is?"

"Of course it is." He smiled down at her, then leaning forward, he whispered, "This time we're going to do it right."

It was a warm evening in late July as Callie stepped out of her parents' farmhouse to the porch, where her father was waiting in the twilight.

Walter Woodville turned then gasped as he saw his eldest daughter in her wedding gown. "You look beautiful, pumpkin."

Callie looked down shyly at the 1950s-style, tea-length gown in ivory lace. "Thanks to Mom. She did the alterations from Grandma's dress."

"Your Mama always makes everything beautiful. And so do you." Tears rose to his eyes as he whispered, "I'm so proud to be your father." His voice was suspiciously rough. Clearing his throat, he held out his arm. "Are you ready?"

She walked with him the short distance across the gravel driveway. The rising moon glowed across the wide ocean of her father's barley fields. The night was quiet and magical. Fireflies glowed through the sapphire night. As they went toward the barn, she could hear the cicadas at a distance, but even their eerie singing wasn't enough to drown the loud drumbeat of her heart.

Clutching her father's arm with one hand, and a bouquet of bright pink Gerbera daisies in the other, Callie looked back at the farmhouse. Her childhood home was a little careworn, with yellow paint peeling in spots. But it was snug and warm and full of good memories. She looked at the swing on the porch, at her mother's red flowers in pots. So many memories. So much love.

"I just hope we do everything right," she whispered.

Her father smiled. "You won't."

"Then I hope we do half as well as you and Mom."

He put his hand over hers, his craggy face sparkling with tears. "You will. You two were made for each other. He's a good one," he said gruffly.

Callie resisted the urge to laugh. Her father had a new appreciation for Eduardo since their three days up at the fishing cabin in Wisconsin. Any man who could face Callie's father, her four uncles and six male cousins, and Brandon, all with guns and hunting bows, was clearly man enough to be Walter's son-in-law. The way Eduardo had humbly asked permission for his daughter's hand in marriage hadn't hurt, either.

Somehow, even Brandon and Eduardo had managed to bury the hatchet. The story she heard afterward was a

bit muddled, but apparently while they were at the cabin
Brandon had nearly shot Eduardo in the foot with his hunting rifle. Callie was rather dubious about how this equaled
friendship, but afterward the two men had drunk beer
around the campfire. "Marrying you two Woodville sisters, we realized we needed to be allies," Eduardo said
with a grin, and Callie wasn't sure whether she should be
offended or not.

Eduardo had won Jane's approval even more easily,
simply through his vigorous appreciation for her cooking
and fruit pies. "Although," her mother had said coyly, "a
few more grandchildren wouldn't hurt."

Eduardo had looked at Callie with a wicked grin, even
as his voice said meekly, "Yes, ma'am."

At the thought, Callie's eyes welled up. She was finally
sure about a question that had distracted her for days. She
could hardly wait to tell Eduardo...

"Don't cry!" her father said, aghast. He pulled a hand-
kerchief from his coat to dab at the corner of her eye. "Your
mother would never forgive me if she thought I said something that smeared your makeup."

"I'm not crying," Callie wept. Blinking back tears of
his own, he patted her hand and led her past the outdoor
reception area, which had a temporary dance floor lit up
by torches and surrounded by coolers full of beer and the
finest champagne. They reached the barn, and Callie stood
in the huge open doorway in her wedding gown beside her
father, who was beaming with pride.

The music on the guitar changed to an acoustic version
of the Bridal March. All at once, her friends and family
rose from the benches used as makeshift pews, gasping
as they stared at Callie.

But she had eyes only for Eduardo.

He stood at the end of the aisle, handsome in a vintage

suit. His dark eyes lit up when he saw her, and he looked dazzled. He was flanked by the best man and maid of honor, who themselves were planning to wed in just two months' time. Sami's leg still hadn't completely healed, and she used a crutch, but she glowed with happiness. So did Brandon, every time he looked at her. He'd cheered Sami throughout her hospital stay by talking about the small farm they would buy once they wed, using the insurance check from the wrecked Rolls-Royce. Callie felt a lump in her throat as she looked at two of the people she loved most in the world, who were both happy at last.

And so was she.

Today, she would marry her best friend. But Eduardo wasn't just her best friend. He was her soul mate, her lover, the man she trusted, the father of her child. The man she wanted to sleep with every night. The man she wanted to wake up to every morning. The man she wanted to fight with, to make love to. The man she wanted to yell at and laugh with. The man she wanted to love for the rest of her life. Her partner.

"Dearly beloved," the parson began, "we are gathered here today…"

As he spoke the magical words that would make them once again man and wife, Callie looked at her once and future husband. Swaying lanterns glowed above them in vivid colors as Eduardo looked down at her. Love illuminated his chiseled, angular face. His dark eyes were deep with devotion.

"Who gives this woman to be married to this man?"

"Her mother and I do," Walter said, and Callie heard the tremble beneath his rough voice, felt the shake of his burly arm as he handed her over to Eduardo's keeping. Kissing her father's cheek, Callie smiled down at her mother in the front row, who held baby Marisol in her lap.

As the parson spoke the wedding homily, Callie listened to the soft wind against the barley. She heard the creak of the old barn around them as Eduardo spoke his wedding vows, and the low timbre of his voice reverberated through her soul. She felt the strength of his powerful, gentle hand as he slid a plain gold band on her finger, simple and special and eternal. Just like their growing family.

Callie hid a smile. She could hardly wait to tell him that he wasn't just becoming her husband again, but a father again, too. Their baby was due in February. Perhaps she would whisper the news in his ear during their first dance, while they swayed together surrounded by flickering torches, beneath a sky so wide it stretched forever. Maybe they'd spend the summer here, autumn in New York, winter in Spain. Their love crossed oceans. But when it was time for her baby to be born, she knew there was only one place she wanted to be. Home.

And as she looked up at Eduardo, that's exactly where she was. In his arms, she was home. No matter where their lives took them.

"And do you, Calliope Marlena Woodville, take this man to be your lawfully wedded husband, for better or for worse, for richer or for poorer, to love and cherish from this day forward, until death do you part?"

In the breathless hush, Callie glanced back at her baby, at her family and friends in the old barn. It was exactly like she'd always imagined it would be. Closing her eyes, Callie took a deep breath, remembering all the impossible dreams she'd had as a girl.

Then, opening her eyes, Callie turned back to Eduardo, and spoke the two words that made all those dreams come true.

* * * * *

Mills & Boon® Hardback

July 2012

ROMANCE

The Secrets She Carried	Lynne Graham
To Love, Honour and Betray	Jennie Lucas
Heart of a Desert Warrior	Lucy Monroe
Unnoticed and Untouched	Lynn Raye Harris
A Royal World Apart	Maisey Yates
Distracted by her Virtue	Maggie Cox
The Count's Prize	Christina Hollis
The Tarnished Jewel of Jazaar	Susanna Carr
Keeping Her Up All Night	Anna Cleary
The Rules of Engagement	Ally Blake
Argentinian in the Outback	Margaret Way
The Sheriff's Doorstep Baby	Teresa Carpenter
The Sheikh's Jewel	Melissa James
The Rebel Rancher	Donna Alward
Always the Best Man	Fiona Harper
How the Playboy Got Serious	Shirley Jump
Sydney Harbour Hospital: Marco's Temptation	Fiona McArthur
Dr Tall, Dark...and Dangerous?	Lynne Marshall

MEDICAL

The Legendary Playboy Surgeon	Alison Roberts
Falling for Her Impossible Boss	Alison Roberts
Letting Go With Dr Rodriguez	Fiona Lowe
Waking Up With His Runaway Bride	Louisa George

ROMANCE

Roccanti's Marriage Revenge	Lynne Graham
The Devil and Miss Jones	Kate Walker
Sheikh Without a Heart	Sandra Marton
Savas's Wildcat	Anne McAllister
A Bride for the Island Prince	Rebecca Winters
The Nanny and the Boss's Twins	Barbara McMahon
Once a Cowboy...	Patricia Thayer
When Chocolate Is Not Enough...	Nina Harrington

HISTORICAL

The Mysterious Lord Marlowe	Anne Herries
Marrying the Royal Marine	Carla Kelly
A Most Unladylike Adventure	Elizabeth Beacon
Seduced by Her Highland Warrior	Michelle Willingham

MEDICAL

The Boss She Can't Resist	Lucy Clark
Heart Surgeon, Hero...Husband?	Susan Carlisle
Dr Langley: Protector or Playboy?	Joanna Neil
Daredevil and Dr Kate	Leah Martyn
Spring Proposal in Swallowbrook	Abigail Gordon
Doctor's Guide to Dating in the Jungle	Tina Beckett

Mills & Boon® Hardback

August 2012

ROMANCE

Contract with Consequences	Miranda Lee
The Sheikh's Last Gamble	Trish Morey
The Man She Shouldn't Crave	Lucy Ellis
The Girl He'd Overlooked	Cathy Williams
A Tainted Beauty	Sharon Kendrick
One Night With The Enemy	Abby Green
The Dangerous Jacob Wilde	Sandra Marton
His Last Chance at Redemption	Michelle Conder
The Hidden Heart of Rico Rossi	Kate Hardy
Marrying the Enemy	Nicola Marsh
Mr Right, Next Door!	Barbara Wallace
The Cowboy Comes Home	Patricia Thayer
The Rancher's Housekeeper	Rebecca Winters
Her Outback Rescuer	Marion Lennox
Monsoon Wedding Fever	Shoma Narayanan
If the Ring Fits...	Jackie Braun
Sydney Harbour Hospital: Ava's Re-Awakening	Carol Marinelli
How To Mend A Broken Heart	Amy Andrews

MEDICAL

Falling for Dr Fearless	Lucy Clark
The Nurse He Shouldn't Notice	Susan Carlisle
Every Boy's Dream Dad	Sue MacKay
Return of the Rebel Surgeon	Connie Cox

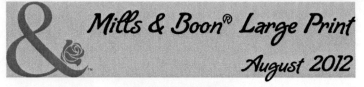

Mills & Boon® Large Print

August 2012

ROMANCE

A Deal at the Altar	Lynne Graham
Return of the Moralis Wife	Jacqueline Baird
Gianni's Pride	Kim Lawrence
Undone by His Touch	Annie West
The Cattle King's Bride	Margaret Way
New York's Finest Rebel	Trish Wylie
The Man Who Saw Her Beauty	Michelle Douglas
The Last Real Cowboy	Donna Alward
The Legend of de Marco	Abby Green
Stepping out of the Shadows	Robyn Donald
Deserving of His Diamonds?	Melanie Milburne

HISTORICAL

The Scandalous Lord Lanchester	Anne Herries
Highland Rogue, London Miss	Margaret Moore
His Compromised Countess	Deborah Hale
The Dragon and the Pearl	Jeannie Lin
Destitute On His Doorstep	Helen Dickson

MEDICAL

Sydney Harbour Hospital: Lily's Scandal	Marion Lennox
Sydney Harbour Hospital: Zoe's Baby	Alison Roberts
Gina's Little Secret	Jennifer Taylor
Taming the Lone Doc's Heart	Lucy Clark
The Runaway Nurse	Dianne Drake
The Baby Who Saved Dr Cynical	Connie Cox